I0764314

The Point of Honor

A MILITARY TALE

The Point of Honor

A MILITARY TALE

JOSEPH CONRAD

ÆGYPAN PRESS

1908

The Point of Honor
A publication of
ÆGYPAN PRESS

www.aegypan.com

I

Napoleon the First, whose career had the quality of a duel against the whole of Europe, disliked dueling between the officers of his army. The great military emperor was not a swashbuckler, and had little respect for tradition.

Nevertheless, a story of dueling which became a legend in the army runs through the epic of imperial wars. To the surprise and admiration of their fellows, two officers, like insane artists trying to gild refined gold or paint the lily, pursued their private contest through the years of universal carnage. They were officers of cavalry, and their connection with the high-spirited but fanciful animal which carries men into battle seems particularly appropriate. It would be difficult to imagine for heroes of this legend two officers of infantry of the fine, for example, whose fantasy is tamed by much walking exercise and whose valor necessarily must be of a more plodding kind. As to artillery, or engineers whose heads are kept cool on a diet of mathematics, it is simply unthinkable.

The names of the two officers were Feraud and D'Hubert, and they were both lieutenants in a regiment of hussars, but not in the same regiment.

Feraud was doing regimental work, but Lieutenant D'Hubert had the good fortune to be attached to the person of the general commanding the division, as *officier d'ordonnance.* It was in Strasbourg, and in this agreeable and important garrison, they were enjoying greatly a short interval of peace. They were enjoying it, though both intensely warlike, because it was a sword-sharpening, firelock-cleaning peace dear to a military heart and undamaging to military prestige inasmuch that no one believed in its sincerity or duration.

Under those historical circumstances so favorable to the proper appreciation of military leisure Lieutenant D'Hubert could have been seen one fine afternoon making his way along the street of a cheerful suburb towards Lieutenant Feraud's quarters, which were in a private house with a garden at the back, belonging to an old maiden lady.

His knock at the door was answered instantly by a young maid in Alsatian costume. Her fresh complexion and her long eyelashes, which she lowered modestly at the sight of the tall officer, caused Lieutenant D'Hubert, who was accessible to esthetic impressions, to relax the cold, on-duty expression of his face. At the same time he observed that the girl had over her arm a pair of hussar's breeches, red with a blue stripe.

"Lieutenant Feraud at home?" he inquired benevolently.

"Oh, no, sir. He went out at six this morning."

And the little maid tried to close the door, but Lieutenant D'Hubert, opposing this move with gentle firmness, stepped into the anteroom jingling his spurs.

"Come, my dear. You don't mean to say he has not been home since six o'clock this morning?"

Saying these words, Lieutenant D'Hubert opened without ceremony the door of a room so comfortable and neatly ordered that only from internal evidence in the shape of boots, uniforms and military accoutrements, did he acquire the conviction that it was Lieutenant Feraud's room. And he saw also that Lieutenant Feraud was not at home. The truthful maid had followed him and looked up inquisitively.

"H'm," said Lieutenant D'Hubert, greatly disappointed, for he had already visited all the haunts where a lieutenant of hussars could be found of a fine afternoon. "And do you happen to know, my dear, why he went out at six this morning?"

"No," she answered readily. "He came home late at night and snored. I heard him when I got up at five. Then he dressed himself in his oldest uniform and went out. Service, I suppose."

"Service? Not a bit of it!" cried Lieutenant D'Hubert. "Learn, my child, that he went out so early to fight a duel with a civilian."

She heard the news without a quiver of her dark eyelashes. It was very obvious that the actions of Lieutenant Feraud were generally above criticism. She only looked up for a moment in mute surprise, and Lieutenant D'Hubert concluded from this absence of emotion that she must have seen Lieutenant Feraud since the morning. He looked around the room.

"Come," he insisted, with confidential familiarity. "He's perhaps somewhere in the house now?"

She shook her head.

"So much the worse for him," continued Lieutenant D'Hubert, in a tone of anxious conviction. "But he has been home this morning?"

This time the pretty maid nodded slightly.

"He has!" cried Lieutenant D'Hubert. "And went out again? What for? Couldn't he keep quietly indoors? What a lunatic! My dear child. . . ."

Lieutenant D'Hubert's natural kindness of disposition and strong sense of comradeship helped his powers of observation, which generally were not remarkable. He changed his tone to a most insinuating softness; and gazing at the hussar's breeches hanging over the arm of the girl, he appealed to the interest she took in Lieutenant Feraud's comfort and happiness. He was pressing and persuasive. He used his eyes, which were large and fine, with excellent effect. His anxiety to get hold at once of Lieutenant Feraud, for Lieutenant Feraud's own good, seemed so genuine that at last it overcame the girl's discretion. Unluckily she had not much to tell. Lieutenant Feraud had returned home shortly before ten; had walked straight into his room and had thrown himself on his bed to resume his slumbers. She had heard him snore rather louder than before far into the afternoon. Then he got up, put on his best uniform and went out. That was all she knew.

She raised her candid eyes up to Lieutenant D'Hubert, who stared at her incredulously.

"It's incredible. Gone parading the town in his best uniform! My dear child, don't you know that he ran that civilian through this morning? Clean through as you spit a hare."

She accepted this gruesome intelligence without any signs of distress. But she pressed her lips together thoughtfully.

"He isn't parading the town," she remarked, in a low tone. "Far from it."

"The civilian's family is making an awful row," continued Lieutenant D'Hubert, pursuing his train of thought. "And the general is very angry. It's one of the best families in the town. Feraud ought to have kept close at least. . . ."

"What will the general do to him?" inquired the girl anxiously.

"He won't have his head cut off, to be sure," answered Lieutenant D'Hubert. "But his conduct is positively indecent. He's making no end of trouble for himself by this sort of bravado."

"But he isn't parading the town," the maid murmured again.

"Why, yes! Now I think of it. I haven't seen him anywhere. What on earth has he done with himself?"

"He's gone to pay a call," suggested the maid, after a moment of silence.

Lieutenant D'Hubert was surprised. "A call! Do you mean a call on a lady? The cheek of the man. But how do you know this?"

Without concealing her woman's scorn for the denseness of the masculine mind, the pretty maid reminded him that Lieutenant Feraud had arrayed himself in his best uniform before going out. He had also put on his newest dolman, she added in a tone as if this conversation were getting on her nerves and turned away brusquely. Lieutenant D'Hubert, without questioning the accuracy of the implied deduction, did not see that it advanced him much on his official quest. For his quest after Lieutenant Feraud had an official character. He did not know any of the women this fellow who had run a man through in the morning was likely to call on in the afternoon. The two officers knew each other but slightly. He bit his gloved finger in perplexity.

"Call!" he exclaimed. "Call on the devil." The girl, with her back to him and folding the hussar's breeches on a chair, said with a vexed little laugh:

"Oh, no! On Madame de Lionne." Lieutenant D'Hubert whistled softly. Madame de Lionne, the wife of a high official, had a well-known salon and some pretensions to sensibility and elegance. The husband was a civilian and old, but the society of the salon was young and military for the greater part. Lieutenant

D'Hubert had whistled, not because the idea of pursuing Lieutenant Feraud into that very salon was in the least distasteful to him, but because having but lately arrived in Strasbourg he had not the time as yet to get an introduction to Madame de Lionne. And what was that swashbuckler Feraud doing there? He did not seem the sort of man who . . .

"Are you certain of what you say?" asked Lieutenant D'Hubert.

The girl was perfectly certain. Without turning round to look at him she explained that the coachman of their next-door neighbors knew the *maître-d'hôtel* of Madame de Lionne. In this way she got her information. And she was perfectly certain. In giving this assurance she sighed. Lieutenant Feraud called there nearly every afternoon.

"Ah, bah!" exclaimed D'Hubert ironically. His opinion of Madame de Lionne went down several degrees. Lieutenant Feraud did not seem to him specially worthy of attention on the part of a woman with a reputation for sensibility and elegance. But there was no saying. At bottom they were all alike – very practical rather than idealistic. Lieutenant D'Hubert, however, did not allow his mind to dwell on these considerations. "By thunder!" he reflected aloud. "The general goes there sometimes. If he happens to find the fellow making eyes at the lady there will be the devil to pay. Our general is not a very accommodating person, I can tell you."

"Go quickly then. Don't stand here now I've told you where he is," cried the girl, coloring to the eyes.

"Thanks, my dear. I don't know what I would have done without you."

After manifesting his gratitude in an aggressive way which at first was repulsed violently and then submitted to with a sudden and still more repellent indifference, Lieutenant D'Hubert took his departure.

He clanked and jingled along the streets with a martial swagger. To run a comrade to earth in a drawing room where he was not known did not trouble him in the least. A uniform is a social passport. His position as *officier d'ordonnance* of the general added to his assurance. Moreover, now he knew where to find Lieutenant Feraud, he had no option. It was a service matter.

Madame de Lionne's house had an excellent appearance. A man in livery opening the door of a large drawing room with a waxed floor, shouted his name and stood aside to let him pass. It was a reception day. The ladies wearing hats surcharged with a profusion of feathers, sheathed in clinging white gowns from their armpits to the tips of their low satin shoes, looked sylphlike and cool in a great display of bare necks and arms. The men who talked with them, on the contrary, were arrayed heavily in ample, colored garments with stiff collars up to their ears and thick sashes round their waists. Lieutenant D'Hubert made his unabashed way across the room, and bowing low before a sylphlike form reclining on a couch, offered his apologies for this intrusion, which nothing could excuse but the extreme urgency of the service order he had to communicate to his comrade Feraud. He proposed to himself to come presently in a more regular manner and beg forgiveness for interrupting this interesting conversation. . . .

A bare arm was extended to him with gracious condescension even before he had finished speaking. He pressed the hand respectfully to his lips and made the mental remark that it was bony. Madame de Lionne was a blonde with too fine a skin and a long face.

"C'est ça!" she said, with an ethereal smile, disclosing a set of large teeth. "Come this evening to plead for

your forgiveness."

"I will not fail, madame."

Meantime Lieutenant Feraud, splendid in his new dolman and the extremely polished boots of his calling, sat on a chair within a foot of the couch and, one hand propped on his thigh, with the other twirled his moustache to a point without uttering a sound. At a significant glance from D'Hubert he rose without alacrity and followed him into the recess of a window.

"What is it you want with me?" he asked in a tone of annoyance, which astonished not a little the other. Lieutenant D'Hubert could not imagine that in the innocence of his heart and simplicity of his conscience Lieutenant Feraud took a view of his duel in which neither remorse nor yet a rational apprehension of consequences had any place. Though Lieutenant Feraud had no clear recollection how the quarrel had originated (it was begun in an establishment where beer and wine are drunk late at night), he had not the slightest doubt of being himself the outraged party. He had secured two experienced friends or his seconds. Everything had been done according to the rules governing that sort of adventure. And a duel is obviously fought for the purpose of someone being at least hurt if not killed outright. The civilian got hurt. That also was in order. Lieutenant Feraud was perfectly tranquil. But Lieutenant D'Hubert mistook this simple attitude for affectation and spoke with some heat.

"I am directed by the general to give you the order to go at once to your quarters and remain there under close arrest."

It was now the turn of Lieutenant Feraud to be astonished.

"What the devil are you telling me there?" he murmured faintly, and fell into such profound wonder that he could only follow mechanically the motions of

Lieutenant D'Hubert. The two officers – one tall, with an interesting face and a moustache the color of ripe corn, the other short and sturdy, with a hooked nose and a thick crop of black, curly hair – approached the mistress of the house to take their leave. Madame de Lionne, a woman of eclectic taste, smiled upon these armed young men with impartial sensibility and an equal share of interest. Madame de Lionne took her delight in the infinite variety of the human species. All the eyes in the drawing room followed the departing officers, one strutting, the other striding, with curiosity. When the door had closed after them one or two men who had already heard of the duel imparted the information to the sylphlike ladies, who received it with little shrieks of humane concern.

Meantime the two hussars walked side by side, Lieutenant Feraud trying to fathom the hidden reason of things which in this instance eluded the grasp of his intellect; Lieutenant D'Hubert feeling bored by the part he had to play; because the general's instructions were that he should see personally that Lieutenant Feraud carried out his orders to the letter and at once.

"The chief seems to know this animal," he thought, eyeing his companion, whose round face, the round eyes and even the twisted-up jet black little moustache seemed animated by his mental exasperation before the incomprehensible. And aloud he observed rather reproachfully, "The general is in a devilish fury with you."

Lieutenant Feraud stopped short on the edge of the pavement and cried in the accents of unmistakable sincerity: "What on earth for?" The innocence of the fiery Gasçon soul was depicted in the manner in which he seized his head in both his hands as if to prevent it bursting with perplexity.

"For the duel," said Lieutenant D'Hubert curtly. He

was annoyed greatly by this sort of perverse fooling.

"The duel! The . . ."

Lieutenant Feraud passed from one paroxysm of astonishment into another. He dropped his hands and walked on slowly trying to reconcile this information with the state of his own feelings. It was impossible. He burst out indignantly:

"Was I to let that sauerkraut-eating civilian wipe his boots on the uniform of the Seventh Hussars?"

Lieutenant D'Hubert could not be altogether unsympathetic toward that sentiment. This little fellow is a lunatic, he thought to himself, but there is something in what he says.

"Of course, I don't know how far you were justified," he said soothingly. "And the general himself may not be exactly informed. A lot of people have been deafening him with their lamentations."

"Ah, he is not exactly informed," mumbled Lieutenant Feraud, walking faster and faster as his choler at the injustice of his fate began to rise. "He is not exactly. . . . And he orders me under close arrest with God knows what afterward."

"Don't excite yourself like this," remonstrated the other. "That young man's people are very influential, you know, and it looks bad enough on the face of it. The general had to take notice of their complaint at once. I don't think he means to be oversevere with you. It is best for you to be kept out of sight for a while."

"I am very much obliged to the general," muttered Lieutenant Feraud through his teeth.

"And perhaps you would say I ought to be grateful to you too for the trouble you have taken to hunt me up in the drawing room of a lady who . . ."

"Frankly," interrupted Lieutenant D'Hubert, with an innocent laugh, "I think you ought to be. I had no end of trouble to find out where you were. It wasn't exactly the place for you to disport yourself in under the circumstances. If the general had caught you there making eyes at the goddess of the temple. . . . Oh, my word. . . ! He hates to be bothered with complaints against his officers, you know. And it looked uncommonly like sheer bravado."

The two officers had arrived now at the street door of Lieutenant Feraud's lodgings. The latter turned toward his companion. "Lieutenant D'Hubert," he said, "I have something to say to you which can't be said very well in the street. You can't refuse to come in."

The pretty maid had opened the door. Lieutenant Feraud brushed past her brusquely and she raised her scared, questioning eyes to Lieutenant D'Hubert, who could do nothing but shrug his shoulders slightly as he followed with marked reluctance.

In his room Lieutenant Feraud unhooked the clasp, flung his new dolman on the bed, and folding his arms across his chest, turned to the other hussar.

"Do you imagine I am a man to submit tamely to injustice?" he inquired in a boisterous voice.

"Oh, do be reasonable," remonstrated Lieutenant D'Hubert.

"I am reasonable. I am perfectly reasonable," retorted the other, ominously lowering his voice. "I can't call the general to account for his behavior, but you are going to answer to me for yours."

"I can't listen to this nonsense," murmured Lieutenant D'Hubert, making a slightly contemptuous grimace.

"You call that nonsense. It seems to me perfectly clear. Unless you don't understand French."

"What on earth do you mean?"

"I mean," screamed suddenly Lieutenant Feraud, "to cut off your ears to teach you not to disturb me, orders or no orders, when I am talking to a lady."

A profound silence followed this mad declaration – and through the open window Lieutenant D'Hubert heard the little birds singing sanely in the garden. He said coldly:

"Why! If you take that tone, of course I will hold myself at your disposal whenever you are at liberty to attend to this affair. But I don't think you will cut off my ears."

"I am going to attend to it at once," declared Lieutenant Feraud, with extreme truculence. "If you are thinking of displaying your airs and graces tonight in Madame de Lionne's salon you are very much mistaken."

"Really," said Lieutenant D'Hubert, who was beginning to feel irritated, "you are an impracticable sort of fellow. The general's orders to me were to put you under arrest, not to carve you into small pieces. Good-morning." Turning his back on the little Gasçon who, always sober in his potations, was as though born intoxicated, with the sunshine of his wine-ripening country, the northman, who could drink hard on occasion, but was born sober under the watery skies of Picardy, made calmly for the door. Hearing, however, the unmistakable sound, behind his back, of a sword drawn from the scabbard, he had no option but to stop.

"Devil take this mad Southerner," he thought, spinning round and surveying with composure the warlike posture of Lieutenant Feraud with the unsheathed sword in his hand.

"At once. At once," stuttered Feraud, beside himself.

"You had my answer," said the other, keeping his temper very well.

At first he had been only vexed and somewhat amused. But now his face got clouded. He was asking himself seriously how he could manage to get away.

Obviously it was impossible to run from a man with a sword, and as to fighting him, it seemed completely out of the question.

He waited awhile, then said exactly what was in his heart:

"Drop this; I won't fight you now. I won't be made ridiculous."

"Ah, you won't!" hissed the Gasçon. "I suppose you prefer to be made infamous. Do you hear what I say. . . ? Infamous! Infamous! Infamous!" he shrieked, raising and falling on his toes and getting very red in the face. Lieutenant D'Hubert, on the contrary, became very pale at the sound of the unsavory word, then flushed pink to the roots of his fair hair.

"But you can't go out to fight; you are under arrest, you lunatic," he objected, with angry scorn.

"There's the garden. It's big enough to lay out your long carcass in," spluttered out Lieutenant Feraud with such ardor that somehow the anger of the cooler man subsided.

"This is perfectly absurd," he said, glad enough to think he had found a way out of it for the moment. "We will never get any of our comrades to serve as seconds. It's preposterous."

"Seconds! Damn the seconds! We don't want any seconds. Don't you worry about any seconds. I will send word to your friends to come and bury you when I am done. This is no time for ceremonies. And if you want any witnesses, I'll send word to the old girl to put her head out of a window at the back. Stay! There's the gardener. He'll do. He's as deaf as a post, but he has two eyes in his head. Come along. I will teach you, my staff officer, that the carrying about of a general's orders is not always child's play."

While thus discoursing he had unbuckled his empty scabbard. He sent it flying under the bed, and, lowering the point of the sword, brushed past the perplexed Lieutenant D'Hubert, crying: "Follow me." Directly he had flung open the door a faint shriek was heard, and the pretty maid, who had been listening at the keyhole, staggered backward, putting the backs of her hands over her eyes. He didn't seem to see her, but as he was crossing the anteroom she ran after him and seized his left arm. He shook her off and then she rushed upon Lieutenant D'Hubert and clawed at the sleeve of his uniform.

"Wretched man," she sobbed despairingly. "Is this what you wanted to find him for?"

"Let me go," entreated Lieutenant D'Hubert, trying to disengage himself gently. "It's like being in a madhouse," he protested with exasperation. "Do let me go, I won't do him any harm."

A fiendish laugh from Lieutenant Feraud commented that assurance. "Come along," he cried impatiently, with a stamp of his foot.

And Lieutenant D'Hubert did follow. He could do nothing else. But in vindication of his sanity it must be recorded that as he passed out of the anteroom the notion of opening the street door and bolting out presented itself to this brave youth, only, of course, to be instantly dismissed: for he felt sure that the other would pursue him without shame or compunction. And the prospect of an officer of hussars being chased along the street by another officer of hussars with a naked sword could not be for a moment entertained. Therefore he followed into the garden. Behind them the girl tottered out too. With ashy lips and wild, scared eyes, she surrendered to a dreadful curiosity. She had also a vague notion of rushing, if need be, between Lieutenant Feraud and death.

The deaf gardener, utterly unconscious of approaching footsteps, went on watering his flowers till Lieutenant Feraud thumped him on the back. Beholding suddenly an infuriated man, flourishing a big saber, the old chap, trembling in all his limbs, dropped the watering pot. At once Lieutenant Feraud kicked it away with great animosity; then seizing the gardener by the throat, backed him against a tree and held him there shouting in his ear:

"Stay here and look on. You understand you've got to look on. Don't dare budge from the spot."

Lieutenant D'Hubert, coming slowly down the walk, unclasped his dolman with undisguised reluctance. Even then, with his hand already on his sword, he hesitated to draw, till a roar *"En garde, fichtre!* What do you think you came here for?" and the rush of his adversary forced him to put himself as quickly as possible in a posture of defense.

The angry clash of arms filled that prim garden, which hitherto had known no more warlike sound than the click of clipping shears; and presently the upper part of an old lady's body was projected out of a window upstairs. She flung her arms above her white cap, and began scolding in a thin, cracked voice. The gardener remained glued to the tree looking on, his toothless mouth open in idiotic astonishment, and a little farther up the walk the pretty girl, as if held by a spell, ran to and fro on a small grass plot, wringing her hands and muttering crazily. She did not rush between the combatants. The onslaughts of Lieutenant Feraud were so fierce that her heart failed her.

Lieutenant D'Hubert, his faculties concentrated upon defense, needed all his skill and science of the sword to stop the rushes of his adversary. Twice already he had had to break ground.

It bothered him to feel his foothold made insecure by the round dry gravel of the path rolling under the hard soles of his boots. This was most unsuitable ground, he thought, keeping a watchful, narrowed gaze shaded by long eyelashes upon the fiery staring eyeballs of his thickset adversary. This absurd affair would ruin his reputation of a sensible, steady, promising young officer. It would damage, at any rate, his immediate prospects and lose him the good will of his general. These worldly preoccupations were no doubt misplaced in view of the solemnity of the moment. For a duel whether regarded as a ceremony in the cult of honor or even when regrettably casual and reduced in its moral essence to a distinguished form of manly sport, demands perfect singleness of intention, a homicidal austerity of mood. On the other hand, this vivid concern for the future in a man occupied in keeping sudden death at sword's length from his breast, had not a bad effect, inasmuch as it began to rouse the slow anger of Lieutenant D'Hubert. Some seventy seconds had elapsed since they had crossed steel and Lieutenant D'Hubert had to break ground again in order to avoid impaling his reckless adversary like a beetle for a cabinet of specimens. The result was that, misapprehending the motive, Lieutenant Feraud, giving vent to triumphant snarls, pressed his attack with renewed vigor.

This enraged animal, thought D'Hubert, will have me against the wall directly. He imagined himself much closer to the house than he was; and he dared not turn his head, such an act under the circumstances being equivalent to deliberate suicide. It seemed to him that he was keeping his adversary off with his eyes much more than with his point. Lieutenant Feraud crouched and bounded with a tigerish, ferocious agility – enough to trouble the stoutest heart. But what was more appalling than the fury of a wild beast accomplishing in all innocence of heart a natural function, was the fixity of savage purpose man alone is capable of displaying. Lieutenant D'Hubert in the midst of his worldly preoccupations perceived it at last. It was an absurd and damaging affair to be drawn into. But whatever silly intention the fellow had started with, it was clear that by this time he meant to kill – nothing else. He meant it with an intensity of will utterly beyond the inferior faculties of a tiger.

As is the case with constitutionally brave men, the full view of the danger interested Lieutenant D'Hubert. And directly he got properly interested, the length of his arm and the coolness of his head told in his favor. It was the turn of Lieutenant Feraud to recoil. He did this with a blood-curdling grunt of baffled rage. He made a swift feint and then rushed straight forward.

"Ah! you would, would you?" Lieutenant D'Hubert exclaimed mentally to himself. The combat had lasted nearly two minutes, time enough for any man to get embittered, apart from the merits of the quarrel. And all at once it was over. Trying to close breast to breast under his adversary's guard, Lieutenant Feraud received a slash on his shortened arm. He did not feel it in the least, but it checked his rush, and his feet slipping on the gravel, he fell backward with great violence. The shock jarred his boiling brain into the perfect quietude of insensibility. Simultaneously with his fall the pretty servant girl shrieked piercingly; but the old maiden lady at the window ceased her scolding and with great presence of mind began to cross herself.

In the first moment, seeing his adversary lying perfectly still, his face to the sky and his toes turned up, Lieutenant D'Hubert thought he had killed him outright. The impression of having slashed hard enough to cut his man clean in two abode with him for awhile in an exaggerated impression of the right good will he had put into the blow. He went down on his knees by the side of the prostrate body. Discovering that not even the arm was severed, a slight sense of disappointment mingled with the feeling of relief. But, indeed, he did not want the death of that sinner. The affair was ugly enough as it stood. Lieutenant D'Hubert addressed himself at once to the task of stopping the bleeding. In this task it was his fate to be ridiculously impeded by the pretty maid. The girl, filling the garden with cries for help, flung herself upon his defenseless back and, twining her fingers in his hair, tugged at his head. Why she should choose to hinder him at this precise moment he could not in the least understand. He did not try. It was all like a very wicked and harassing dream. Twice, to save himself from being pulled over, he had to rise and throw her off. He did this stoically, without a word, kneeling down again at once to go on with his work. But when the work was done he seized both her arms and held them down. Her cap was half off, her face was red, her eyes glared with crazy boldness. He looked mildly into them while she called him a wretch, a traitor and a murderer many times in succession. This did not annoy him so much as the conviction that in her scurries she had managed to scratch his face abundantly. Ridicule would be added to the scandal of the story. He imagined it making its way through the garrison, through the whole army, with every possible distortion of motive and sentiment and circumstance, spreading a doubt upon the sanity of his conduct and the distinction of his taste even into the very bosom of his honorable family. It was all very well for that fellow Feraud, who had no connections, no family to speak of, and no quality but courage which, anyhow, was a matter of course, and possessed by every single trooper in the whole mass of French cavalry. Still holding the wrists of the girl in a strong grip, Lieutenant D'Hubert looked over his shoulder. Lieutenant Feraud had opened his eyes. He did not move. Like a man just waking from a deep sleep he stared with a drowsy expression at the evening sky.

Lieutenant D'Hubert's urgent shouts to the old gardener produced no effect – not so much as to make him shut his toothless mouth. Then he remembered that the man was stone deaf. All that time the girl, attempting to free her wrists, struggled, not with maidenly coyness but like a sort of pretty dumb fury, not even refraining from kicking his shins now and then. He continued to hold her as if in a vice, his instinct telling him that were he to let her go she would fly at his eyes. But he was greatly humiliated by his position. At last she gave up, more exhausted than appeased, he feared. Nevertheless he attempted to get out of this wicked dream by way of negotiation.

"Listen to me," he said as calmly as he could. "Will you promise to run for a surgeon if I let you go?"

He was profoundly afflicted when, panting, sobbing, and choking, she made it clear that she would do nothing of the kind. On the contrary, her incoherent intentions were to remain in the garden and fight with her nails and her teeth for the protection of the prostrate man. This was horrible.

"My dear child," he cried in despair, "is it possible that you think me capable of murdering a wounded adversary? Is it. . . . Be quiet, you little wildcat, you," he added.

She struggled. A thick sleepy voice said behind him: "What are you up to with that girl?"

Lieutenant Feraud had raised himself on his good arm. He was looking sleepily at his other arm, at the mess of blood on his uniform, at a small red pool on the ground, at his saber lying a foot away on the path. Then he laid himself down gently again to think it all out as far as a thundering headache would permit of mental operations.

Lieutenant D'Hubert released the girl's wrists. She flew away down the path and crouched wildly by the side of the vanquished warrior. The shades of night were falling on the little trim garden with this touching group whence proceeded low murmurs of sorrow and compassion with other feeble sounds of a different character as if an imperfectly awake invalid were trying to swear. Lieutenant D'Hubert went away, too exasperated to care what would happen.

He passed through the silent house and congratulated himself upon the dusk concealing his gory hands and scratched face from the passers-by. But this story could by no means be concealed. He dreaded the discredit and ridicule above everything, and was painfully aware of sneaking through the back streets to his quarters. In one of these quiet side streets the sounds of a flute coming out of the open window of a lighted upstairs room in a modest house interrupted his dismal reflections. It was being played with a deliberate, persevering virtuosity, and through the *fioritures* of the tune one could even hear the thump of the foot beating time on the floor.

Lieutenant D'Hubert shouted a name which was that of an army surgeon whom he knew fairly well. The sounds of the flute ceased and the musician appeared at the window, his instrument still in his hand, peering into the street.

"Who calls? You, D'Hubert! What brings you this way?"

He did not like to be disturbed when he was playing the flute. He was a man whose hair had turned grey already in the thankless task of tying up wounds on battlefields where others reaped advancement and glory.

"I want you to go at once and see Feraud. You know Lieutenant Feraud? He lives down the second street.

It's but a step from here."

"What's the matter with him?"

"Wounded."

"Are you sure?"

"Sure!" cried D'Hubert. "I come from there."

"That's amusing," said the elderly surgeon. Amusing was his favorite word; but the expression of his face when he pronounced it never corresponded. He was a stolid man. "Come in," he added. "I'll get ready in a moment."

"Thanks. I will. I want to wash my hands in your room."

Lieutenant D'Hubert found the surgeon occupied in unscrewing his flute and packing the pieces methodically in a velvet-lined case. He turned his head.

"Water there – in the corner. Your hands do want washing."

"I've stopped the bleeding," said Lieutenant D'Hubert. "But you had better make haste. It's rather more than ten minutes ago, you know."

The surgeon did not hurry his movements.

"What's the matter? Dressing came off? That's amusing. I've been busy in the hospital all day, but somebody has told me that he hadn't a scratch."

"Not the same duel probably," growled moodily Lieutenant D'Hubert, wiping his hands on a coarse towel.

"Not the same. . . . What? Another? It would take the very devil to make me go out twice in one day." He looked narrowly at Lieutenant D'Hubert. "How did you come by that scratched face? Both sides too – and symmetrical. It's amusing."

"Very," snarled Lieutenant D'Hubert. "And you will find his slashed arm amusing too. It will keep both of you amused for quite a long time."

The doctor was mystified and impressed by the

brusque bitterness of Lieutenant D'Hubert's tone. They left the house together, and in the street he was still more mystified by his conduct.

"Aren't you coming with me?" he asked.

"No," said Lieutenant D'Hubert. "You can find the house by yourself. The front door will be open very likely."

"All right. Where's his room?"

"Ground floor. But you had better go right through and look in the garden first."

This astonishing piece of information made the surgeon go off without further parley. Lieutenant D'Hubert regained his quarters nursing a hot and uneasy indignation. He dreaded the chaff of his comrades almost as much as the anger of his superiors. He felt as though he had been entrapped into a damaging exposure. The truth was confoundedly grotesque and embarrassing to justify; putting aside the irregularity of the combat itself which made it come dangerously near a criminal offence. Like all men without much imagination, which is such a help in the processes of reflective thought, Lieutenant D'Hubert became frightfully harassed by the obvious aspects of his predicament. He was certainly glad that he had not killed Lieutenant Feraud outside all rules and without the regular witnesses proper to such a transaction. Uncommonly glad. At the same time he felt as though he would have liked to wring his neck for him without ceremony.

He was still under the sway of these contradictory sentiments when the surgeon amateur of the flute came to see him. More than three days had elapsed. Lieutenant D'Hubert was no longer *officier d'ordonnance* to the general commanding the division. He had been sent back to his regiment. And he was resuming his connection with the soldiers' military family, by being shut up in close confinement not at his own quarters in town, but in a room in the barracks. Owing to the gravity of the incident, he was allowed to see no one. He did not know what had happened, what was being said or what was being thought. The arrival of the surgeon was a most unexpected event to the worried captive. The amateur of the flute began by explaining that he was there only by a special favor of the colonel who had thought fit to relax the general isolation order for this one occasion.

"I represented to him that it would be only fair to give you authentic news of your adversary," he continued. "You'll be glad to hear he's getting better fast."

Lieutenant D'Hubert's face exhibited no conventional signs of gladness. He continued to walk the floor of the dusty bare room.

"Take this chair, doctor," he mumbled.

The doctor sat down.

"This affair is variously appreciated in town and in the army. In fact the diversity of opinions is amusing."

"Is it?" mumbled Lieutenant D'Hubert, tramping steadily from wall to wall. But within himself he marveled that there could be two opinions on the matter. The surgeon continued:

"Of course as the real facts are not known –"

"I should have thought," interrupted D'Hubert, "that the fellow would have put you in possession of the facts."

"He did say something," admitted the other, "the first time I saw him. And, by-the-bye, I did find him in the garden. The thump on the back of his head had made him a little incoherent then. Afterwards he was rather reticent than otherwise."

"Didn't think he would have the grace to be ashamed," grunted D'Hubert, who had stood still for a moment. He resumed his pacing while the doctor murmured.

"It's very amusing. Ashamed? Shame was not exactly his frame of mind. However, you may look at the matter otherwise –"

"What are you talking about? What matter?" asked D'Hubert with a sidelong look at the heavy-faced, grey-haired figure seated on a wooden chair.

"Whatever it is," said the surgeon, "I wouldn't pronounce an opinion on your conduct. . . ."

"By heavens, you had better not," burst out D'Hubert.

"There! There! Don't be so quick in flourishing the sword. It doesn't pay in the long run. Understand once for all that I would not carve any of you youngsters except with the tools of my trade. But my advice is good. Moderate your temper. If you go on like this you will make for yourself an ugly reputation."

"Go on like what?" demanded Lieutenant D'Hubert, stopping short, quite startled. "I! I! make for myself a reputation. . . . What do you imagine –"

"I told you I don't wish to judge of the rights and wrongs of this incident. It's not my business. Nevertheless. . . ."

"What on earth has he been telling you?" interrupted Lieutenant D'Hubert in a sort of awed scare.

"I told, you already that at first when I picked him up in the garden he was incoherent. Afterwards he was naturally reticent. But I gather at least that he could not help himself. . . ."

"He couldn't?" shouted Lieutenant D'Hubert. Then lowering his voice, "And what about me? Could I help myself?"

The surgeon rose. His thoughts were running upon the flute, his constant companion, with a consoling voice. In the vicinity of field ambulances, after twenty-four hours' hard work, he had been known to trouble with its sweet sounds the horrible stillness of battle-fields given over to silence and the dead. The solacing hour of his daily life was approaching and in peace time he held on to the minutes as a miser to his hoard.

"Of course! Of course!" he said perfunctorily. "You would think so. It's amusing. However, being perfectly neutral and friendly to you both, I have consented to deliver his message. Say that I am humoring an invalid if you like. He says that this affair is by no means at an end. He intends to send you his seconds directly he has regained his strength – providing, of course, the army is not in the field at that time."

"He intends – does he? Why certainly," spluttered Lieutenant D'Hubert passionately. The secret of this exasperation was not apparent to the visitor; but this passion confirmed him in the belief which was gaining ground outside that some very serious difference had arisen between these two young men. Something serious enough to wear an air of mystery. Some fact of the utmost gravity. To settle their urgent difference those two young men had risked being broken and disgraced at the outset, almost, of their career. And he feared that the forthcoming inquiry would fail to satisfy the public curiosity. They would not take the public into their confidence as to that something which had passed between them of a nature so outrageous as to make them face a charge of murder – neither more nor less. But what could it be?

The surgeon was not very curious by temperament; but that question, haunting his mind, caused him twice that evening to hold the instrument off his lips and sit silent for a whole minute – right in the middle of a tune – trying to form a plausible conjecture.

II

He succeeded in this object no better than the rest of the garrison and the whole of society. The two young officers, of no especial consequence till then, became distinguished by the universal curiosity as to the origin of their quarrel. Madame de Lionne's salon was the center of ingenious surmises; that lady herself was for a time assailed with inquiries as the last person known to have spoken to these unhappy and reckless young men before they went out together from her house to a savage encounter with swords, at dusk, in a private garden. She protested she had noticed nothing unusual in their demeanor. Lieutenant Feraud had been visibly annoyed at being called away. That was natural enough; no man likes to be disturbed in a conversation with a lady famed for her elegance and sensibility» But, in truth, the subject bored Madame de Lionne since her personality could by no stretch of imagination be connected with this affair. And it irritated her to hear it advanced that there might have been some woman in the case. This irritation arose, not from her elegance or sensibility, but from a more instinctive side of her nature. It became so great at last that she peremptorily forbade the subject to be mentioned under her roof. Near her couch the prohibition was obeyed, but farther off in the salon the pall of the imposed silence continued to be lifted more or less. A diplomatic personage with a long pale face resembling the countenance of a sheep, opined, shaking his head, that it was a quarrel of long standing envenomed by time. It was objected to him that the men themselves were too young for such a theory to fit their proceedings. They belonged also to different and distant parts of France. A subcommissary of the Intendence, an agreeable and cultivated bachelor in keysermere breeches, Hessian boots and a blue coat embroidered with silver lace, who affected to believe in the transmigration of souls, suggested that the two had met perhaps in some previous existence. The feud was in the forgotten past. It might have been something quite inconceivable in the present state of their being; but their souls remembered the animosity and manifested an instinctive antagonism. He developed his theme jocularly. Yet the affair was so absurd from the worldly, the military, the honorable, or the prudential point of view, that this weird explanation seemed rather more reasonable than any other.

The two officers had confided nothing definite to anyone. Resentment, humiliation at having been worsted arms in hand, and an uneasy feeling of having been involved into a scrape by the injustice of fate, kept Lieutenant Feraud savagely dumb. He mistrusted the sympathy of mankind. That would of course go to that dandified staff officer. Lying in bed he raved to himself in his mind or aloud to the pretty maid who ministered to his needs with devotion and listened to his horrible imprecations with alarm. That Lieutenant D'Hubert should be made to "pay for it," whatever it was, seemed to her just and natural. Her principal concern was that Lieutenant Feraud should not excite himself. He appeared so wholly admirable and fascinating to the humility of her heart that her only concern was to see him get well quickly even if it were only to resume his visits to Madame de Lionne's salon.

Lieutenant D'Hubert kept silent for the immediate reason that there was no one except a stupid young soldier servant to speak to. But he was not anxious for the opportunities of which his severe arrest deprived him. He would have been uncommunicative from dread of ridicule. He was aware that the episode, so grave professionally, had its comic side. When reflecting upon it he still felt that he would like to wring Lieutenant Feraud's neck for him. But this formula was figurative rather than precise, and expressed more a state of mind than an actual physical impulse. At the same time there was in that young man a feeling of comradeship and kindness which made him unwilling to make the position of Lieutenant Feraud worse than it was.

He did not want to talk at large about this wretched affair. At the inquiry he would have, of course, to speak the truth in self-defense. This prospect vexed him.

But no inquiry took place. The army took the field instead. Lieutenant D'Hubert, liberated without remark, returned to his regimental duties, and Lieutenant Feraud, his arm still in a sling, rode unquestioned with his squadron to complete his convalescence in the smoke of battlefields and the fresh air of night bivouacs. This bracing treatment suited his case so well that at the first rumor of an armistice being signed he could turn without misgivings to the prosecution of his private warfare.

This time it was to be regular warfare. He dispatched two friends to Lieutenant D'Hubert, whose regiment was stationed only a few miles away. Those friends had asked no questions of their principal. "I must pay him off, that pretty staff officer," he had said grimly, and they went away quite contentedly on their mission. Lieutenant D'Hubert had no difficulty in finding two friends equally discreet and devoted to their principal. "There's a sort of crazy fellow to whom I must give another lesson," he had curtly declared, and they asked for no better reasons.

On these grounds an encounter with dueling swords was arranged one early morning in a convenient field. At the third set-to, Lieutenant D'Hubert found himself lying on his back on the dewy grass, with a hole in his side. A serene sun, rising over a German landscape of meadows and wooded hills, hung on his left. A surgeon – not the flute-player but another – was bending over him, feeling around the wound.

"Narrow squeak. But it will be nothing," he pronounced.

Lieutenant D'Hubert heard these words with pleasure. One of his seconds – the one who, sitting on the wet grass, was sustaining his head on his lap-said:

"The fortune of war, *mon pauvre vieux*. What will you have? You had better make it up, like two good fellows. Do!"

"You don't know what you ask," murmured Lieutenant D'Hubert in a feeble voice. "However, if he . . ."

In another part of the meadow the seconds of Lieutenant Feraud were urging him to go over and shake hands with his adversary.

"You have paid him off now – *que diable*. It's the proper thing to do. This D'Hubert is a decent fellow."

"I know the decency of these generals' pets," muttered Lieutenant Feraud through his teeth for all answer. The somber expression of his face discouraged further efforts at reconciliation. The seconds, bowing from a distance, took their men off the field. In the afternoon, Lieutenant D'Hubert, very popular as a good comrade uniting great bravery with a frank and equable temper, had many visitors. It was remarked that Lieutenant Feraud did not, as customary, show himself much abroad to receive the felicitations of his friends. They would not have failed him, because he, too, was liked for the exuberance of his southern nature and the simplicity of his character. In all the places where officers were in the habit of assembling at the end of the day the duel of the morning was talked over from every point of view. Though Lieutenant D'Hubert had got worsted this time, his swordplay was commended. No one could deny that it was very close, very scientific. If he got touched, some said, it was because he wished to spare his adversary. But by many the vigor and dash of Lieutenant Feraud's attack were pronounced irresistible.

The merits of the two officers as combatants were frankly discussed; but their attitude to each other after the duel was criticized lightly and with caution. It was irreconcilable, and that was to be regretted. After all, they knew best what the care of their honor dictated. It was not a matter for their comrades to pry into overmuch. As to the origin of the quarrel, the general impression was that it dated from the time they were holding garrison in Strasburg. Only the musical surgeon shook his head at that. It went much farther back, he hinted discreetly.

"Why! You must know the whole story," cried several voices, eager with curiosity. "You were there! What was it?"

He raised his eyes from his glass deliberately and said:

"Even if I knew ever so well, you can't expect me to tell you, since both the principals choose to say nothing."

He got up and went out, leaving the sense of mystery

behind him. He could not stay longer because the witching hour of flute-playing was drawing near. After he had gone a very young officer observed solemnly:

"Obviously! His lips are sealed."

Nobody questioned the high propriety of that remark. Somehow it added to the impressiveness of the affair. Several older officers of both regiments, prompted by nothing but sheer kindness and love of harmony, proposed to form a Court of Honor to which the two officers would leave the task of their reconciliation. Unfortunately, they began by approaching Lieutenant Feraud. The assumption was, that having just scored heavily, he would be found placable and disposed to moderation.

The reasoning was sound enough; nevertheless, the move turned out unfortunate. In that relaxation of moral fiber which is brought about by the ease of soothed vanity, Lieutenant Feraud had condescended in the secret of his heart to review the case, and even to doubt not the justice of his cause, but the absolute sagacity of his conduct. This being so, he was disinclined to talk about it. The suggestion of the regimental wise men put him in a difficult position. He was disgusted, and this disgust by a sort of paradoxical logic reawakened his animosity against Lieutenant D'Hubert. Was he to be pestered with this fellow forever – the fellow who had an infernal knack of getting round people somehow? On the other hand, it was difficult to refuse point-blank that sort of mediation sanctioned by the code of honor.

Lieutenant Feraud met the difficulty by an attitude of fierce reserve. He twisted his moustache and used vague words. His case was perfectly clear. He was not ashamed to present it, neither was he afraid to defend it personally. He did not see any reason to jump at the suggestion before ascertaining how his adversary was likely to take it.

Later in the day, his exasperation growing upon him, he was heard in a public place saying sardonically "that it would be the very luckiest thing for Lieutenant D'Hubert, since next time of meeting he need not hope to get off with a mere trifle of three weeks in bed."

This boastful phrase might have been prompted by the most profound Machiavelism. Southern natures often hide under the outward impulsiveness of action and speech a certain amount of astuteness.

Lieutenant Feraud, mistrusting the justice of men, by no means desired a Court of Honor. And these words, according so well with his temperament, had also the merit of serving his turn. Whether meant for that purpose or not, they found their way in less than four-and-twenty hours into Lieutenant D'Hubert's bedroom. In consequence, Lieutenant D'Hubert, sitting propped up with pillows, received the overtures made to him next day by the statement that the affair was of a nature which could not bear discussion.

The pale face of the wounded officer, his weak voice which he had yet to use cautiously, and the courteous dignity of his tone, had a great effect on his hearers. Reported outside, all this did more for deepening the mystery than the vaporings of Lieutenant Feraud. This last was greatly relieved at the issue. He began to enjoy the state of general wonder, and was pleased to add to it by assuming an attitude of moody reserve.

The colonel of Lieutenant D'Hubert's regiment was a grey-haired, weather-beaten warrior who took a simple view of his responsibilities. "I can't" – he thought to himself – "let the best of my subalterns get damaged like this for nothing. I must get to the bottom of this affair privately. He must speak out, if the devil were in it. The colonel should be more than a father to these youngsters." And, indeed, he loved all his men with as much affection as a father of a large family can feel for every individual member of it. If human beings by an oversight of Providence came into the world in the state of civilians, they were born again into a regiment as infants are born into a family, and it was that military birth alone which really counted.

At the sight of Lieutenant D'Hubert standing before him bleached and hollow-eyed, the heart of the old warrior was touched with genuine compassion. All his affection for the regiment – that body of men which he held in his hand to launch forward and draw back, who had given him his rank, ministered to his pride and commanded his thoughts – seemed centered for a moment on the person of the most promising subaltern. He cleared his throat in a threatening manner and frowned terribly.

"You must understand," he began, "that I don't care a rap for the life of a single man in the regiment. You know that I would send the 748 of you men and horses galloping into the pit of perdition with no more compunction than I would kill a fly."

"Yes, colonel. You would be riding at our head," said Lieutenant D'Hubert with a wan smile.

The colonel, who felt the need of being very diplomatic, fairly roared at this.

"I want you to know, Lieutenant D'Hubert, that I could stand aside and see you all riding to Hades, if need be. I am a man to do even that, if the good of the service and my duty to my country required it from me. But that's unthinkable, so don't you even hint at such a thing."

He glared awfully, but his voice became gentle. "There's some milk yet about that moustache of yours, my boy. You don't know what a man like me is capable of. I would hide behind a haystack if . . . Don't grin at me, sir. How dare you? If this were not a private conversation, I would . . . Look here. I am responsible for the proper expenditure of lives under my command for the glory of our country and the honor of the regiment. Do you understand that? Well, then, what the devil do you mean by letting yourself be spitted like this by that fellow of the Seventh Hussars? It's simply disgraceful!"

Lieutenant D'Hubert, who expected another sort of conclusion, felt vexed beyond measure. His shoulders moved slightly. He made no other answer. He could not ignore his responsibility. The colonel softened his glance and lowered his voice.

"It's deplorable," he murmured. And again he changed his tone. "Come," he went on persuasively, but with that note of authority which dwells in the throat of a good leader of men, "this affair must be settled. I desire to be told plainly what it is all about. I demand, as your best friend, to know."

The compelling power of authority, the softening influence of the kindness affected deeply a man just risen from a bed of sickness. Lieutenant D'Hubert's hand, which grasped the knob of a stick, trembled slightly. But his northern temperament, sentimental but cautious and clear-sighted, too, in its idealistic way, predominated over his impulse to make a clean breast of the whole deadly absurdity. According to the precept of transcendental wisdom, he turned his tongue seven times in his mouth before he spoke. He made then only a speech of thanks, nothing more. The colonel listened interested at first, then looked mystified. At last he frowned.

"You hesitate – *mille tonerres!* Haven't I told you that I will condescend to argue with you – as a friend?"

"Yes, colonel," answered Lieutenant D'Hubert softly, "but I am afraid that after you have heard me out as a friend, you will take action as my superior officer."

The attentive colonel snapped his jaws.

"Well, what of that?" he said frankly. "Is it so damnably disgraceful?"

"It is not," negatived Lieutenant D'Hubert in a faint but resolute voice.

"Of course I shall act for the good of the service – nothing can prevent me doing that. What do you think I want to be told for?"

"I know it is not from idle curiosity," tested Lieutenant D'Hubert. "I know you will act wisely. But what about the good fame of the regiment?"

"It cannot be affected by any youthful folly of a lieutenant," the colonel said severely.

"No, it cannot be; but it can be by evil tongues. It will be said that a lieutenant of the Fourth Hussars, afraid of meeting his adversary, is hiding behind his colonel. And that would be worse than hiding behind a haystack – for the good of the service. I cannot afford to do that, colonel."

"Nobody would dare to say anything of the kind," the colonel, beginning very fiercely, ended on an uncertain note. The bravery of Lieutenant D'Hubert was well known; but the colonel was well aware that the dueling courage, the single combat courage, is, rightly or wrongly, supposed to be courage of a special sort; and it was eminently necessary that an officer of his regiment should possess every kind of courage – and prove it, too. The colonel stuck out his lower lip and looked far away with a peculiar glazed stare. This was the expression of his perplexity, an expression practically unknown to his regiment, for perplexity is a sentiment which is incompatible with the rank of colonel of cavalry. The colonel himself was overcome by the unpleasant novelty of the sensation. As he was not accustomed to think except on professional matters connected with the welfare of men and horses and the proper use thereof on the field of glory, his intellectual efforts degenerated into mere mental repetitions of profane language. *"Mille tonerres. . . ! Sacré nom de nom . . ."* he thought.

Lieutenant D'Hubert coughed painfully and went on, in a weary voice:

"There will be plenty of evil tongues to say that I've been cowed. And I am sure you will not expect me to pass that sort of thing over. I may find myself suddenly with a dozen duels on my hands instead of this one affair."

The direct simplicity of this argument came home to the colonel's understanding. He looked at his subordinate fixedly.

"Sit down, lieutenant," he said gruffly. "This is the very devil of a . . . sit down."

"Mon colonel" D'Hubert began again. "I am not afraid of evil tongues. There's a way of silencing them. But there's my peace of mind too. I wouldn't be able to shake off the notion that I've ruined a brother officer. Whatever action you take it is bound to go further. The inquiry has been dropped – let it rest now. It would have been the end of Feraud."

"Hey? What? Did he behave so badly?"

"Yes, it was pretty bad," muttered Lieutenant D'Hubert. Being still very weak, he felt a disposition to cry.

As the other man did not belong to his own regiment the colonel had no difficulty in believing this. He began to pace up and down the room. He was a good chief and a man capable of discreet sympathy. But he was human in other ways, too, and they were apparent because he was not capable of artifice.

"The very devil, lieutenant!" he blurted out in the innocence of his heart, "is that I have declared my intention to get to the bottom of this affair. And when a colonel says something . . . you see . . ."

Lieutenant D'Hubert broke in earnestly.

"Let me entreat you, colonel, to be satisfied with taking my word of honor that I was put into a damnable position where I had no option. I had no choice whatever consistent with my dignity as a man and an officer. . . . After all, colonel, this fact is the very bottom of this affair. Here you've got it. The rest is a mere detail. . . ."

The colonel stopped short. The reputation of Lieutenant D'Hubert for good sense and good temper weighed in the balance. A cool head, a warm heart, open as the day. Always correct in his behavior. One had to trust him. The colonel repressed manfully an immense curiosity.

"H'm! You affirm that as a man and an officer. . . . No option? Eh?"

"As an officer, an officer of the Fourth Hussars, too," repeated Lieutenant D'Hubert, "I had not. And that is the bottom of the affair, colonel."

"Yes. But still I don't see why to one's colonel . . . A colonel is a father – *que diable.*"

Lieutenant D'Hubert ought not to have been allowed out as yet. He was becoming aware of his physical insufficiency with humiliation and despair – but the morbid obstinacy of an invalid possessed him – and at the same time he felt, with dismay, his eyes filling with water. This trouble seemed too big to handle. A tear fell down the thin, pale cheek of Lieutenant D'Hubert. The colonel turned his back on him hastily. You could have heard a pin drop.

"This is some silly woman story – is it not?"

The chief spun round to seize the truth, which is not a beautiful shape living in a well but a shy bird best caught by stratagem. This was the last move of the colonel's diplomacy, and he saw the truth shining unmistakably in the gesture of Lieutenant D'Hubert, raising his weak arms and his eyes to heaven in supreme protest.

"Not a woman affair – eh?" growled the colonel, staring hard. "I don't ask you who or where. All I want to know is whether there is a woman in it?"

Lieutenant D'Hubert's arms dropped and his weak voice was pathetically broken.

"Nothing of the kind, mon colonel."

"On your honor?" insisted the old warrior.

"On my honor."

"Very well," said the colonel thoughtfully, and bit his lip. The arguments of Lieutenant D'Hubert, helped by his liking for the person, had convinced him. Yet it was highly improper that his intervention, of which he had made no secret, should produce no visible effect. He kept Lieutenant D'Hubert a little longer and dismissed him kindly.

"Take a few days more in bed, lieutenant. What the devil does the surgeon mean by reporting you fit for duty?"

On coming out of the colonel's quarters, Lieutenant D'Hubert said nothing to the friend who was waiting outside to take him home. He said nothing to anybody. Lieutenant D'Hubert made no confidences. But in the evening of that day the colonel, strolling under the elms growing near his quarters in the company of his second in command opened his lips.

"I've got to the bottom of this affair," he remarked.

The lieutenant-colonel, a dry brown chip of a man with short side-whiskers, pricked up his ears without letting a sound of curiosity escape him.

"It's no trifle," added the colonel oracularly. The other waited for a long while before he murmured:

"Indeed, sir!"

"No trifle," repeated the colonel, looking straight

before him. "I've, however, forbidden D'Hubert either to send to or receive a challenge from Feraud for the next twelve months."

He had imagined this prohibition to save the prestige a colonel should have. The result of it was to give an official seal to the mystery surrounding this deadly quarrel. Lieutenant D'Hubert repelled by an impassive silence all attempts to worm the truth out of him. Lieutenant Feraud, secretly uneasy at first, regained his assurance as time went on. He disguised his ignorance of the meaning of the imposed truce by little sardonic laughs as though he were amused by what he intended to keep to himself. "But what will you do?" his chums used to ask him. He contented himself by replying, "*Qui vivra verra,*" with a truculent air. And everybody admired his discretion.

Before the end of the truce, Lieutenant D'Hubert got his promotion. It was well earned, but somehow no one seemed to expect the event. When Lieutenant Feraud heard of it at a gathering of officers, he muttered through his teeth, "Is that so?" Unhooking his sword from a peg near the door, he buckled it on carefully and left the company without another word. He walked home with measured steps, struck a light with his flint and steel, and lit his tallow candle. Then, snatching an unlucky glass tumbler off the mantelpiece, he dashed it violently on the floor.

Now that D'Hubert was an officer of a rank superior to his own, there could be no question of a duel. Neither could send nor receive a challenge without rendering himself amenable to a court-martial. It was not to be thought of. Lieutenant Feraud, who for many days now had experienced no real desire to meet Lieutenant D'Hubert arms in hand, chafed at the systematic injustice of fate. "Does he think he will escape me in that way?" he thought indignantly. He saw in it an intrigue, a conspiracy, a cowardly maneuver. That colonel knew what he was doing. He had hastened to recommend his pet for promotion. It was outrageous that a man should be able to avoid the consequences of his acts in such a dark and tortuous manner.

Of a happy-go-lucky disposition, of a temperament more pugnacious than military, Lieutenant Feraud had been content to give and receive blows for sheer love of armed strife and without much thought of advancement. But after this disgusting experience an urgent desire of promotion sprang up in his breast. This fighter by vocation resolved in his mind to seize showy occasions and to court the favorable opinion of his chiefs like a mere worldling. He knew he was as brave as anyone and never doubted his personal charm. It would be easy, he thought. Nevertheless, neither the bravery nor the charm seemed to work very swiftly. Lieutenant Feraud's engaging, careless truculence of a *"beau sabreur"* underwent a change. He began to make bitter allusions to "clever fellows who stick at nothing to get on." The army was full of them, he would say, you had only to look round. And all the time he had in view one person only, his adversary D'Hubert. Once he confided to an appreciative friend: "You see I don't know how to fawn on the right sort of people. It isn't in me."

He did not get his step till a week after Austerlitz. The light cavalry of the *Grande Armée* had its hands very full of interesting work for a little while. But directly the pressure of professional occupation had been eased by the armistice, Captain Feraud took measures to arrange a meeting without loss of time. "I know his tricks," he observed grimly. "If I don't look sharp he will take care to get himself promoted over the heads of a dozen better men than himself. He's got the knack of that sort of thing." This duel was fought in Silesia.

If not fought out to a finish, it was at any rate fought to a standstill. The weapon was the cavalry saber, and the skill, the science, the vigor, and the determination displayed by the adversaries compelled the outspoken admiration of the beholders. It became the subject of talk on both shores of the Danube, and as far south as the garrisons of Gratz and Laybach. They crossed blades seven times. Both had many slight cuts – mere scratches which bled profusely. Both refused to have the combat stopped, time after time, with what appeared the most deadly animosity. This appearance was caused on the part of Captain D'Hubert by a rational desire to be done once for all with this worry; on the part of Feraud by a tremendous exaltation of his pugnacious instincts and the rage of wounded vanity. At last, disheveled, their shirts in rags, covered with gore and hardly able to stand, they were carried forcibly off the field by their marveling and horrified seconds. Later on, besieged by comrades avid of details, these gentlemen declared that they could not have allowed that sort of hacking to go on. Asked whether the quarrel was settled this time, they gave it out as their conviction that it was a difference which could only be settled by one of the parties remaining lifeless on the ground. The sensation spread from army to army corps, and penetrated at last to the smallest detachments of the troops cantoned between the Rhine and the Save. In the cafés in Vienna where the masters of Europe took their ease it was generally estimated from details to hand that the adversaries would be able to meet again in three weeks' time, on the outside. Something really transcendental in the way of dueling was expected.

These expectations were brought to naught by the necessities of the service which separated the two officers. No official notice had been taken of their quarrel.

It was now the property of the army, and not to be meddled with lightly. But the story of the duel, or rather their dueling propensities, must have stood somewhat in the way of their advancement, because they were still captains when they came together again during the war with Prussia. Detached north after Jena with the army commanded by Marshal Bernadotte, Prince of Ponte-Corvo, they entered Lubeck together. It was only after the occupation of that town that Captain Feraud had leisure to consider his future conduct in view of the fact that Captain D'Hubert had been given the position of third aide-de-camp to the marshal. He considered it a great part of a night, and in the morning summoned two sympathetic friends.

"I've been thinking it over calmly," he said, gazing at them with bloodshot, tired eyes. "I see that I must get rid of that intriguing personage. Here he's managed to sneak onto the personal staff of the marshal. It's a direct provocation to me. I can't tolerate a situation in which I am exposed any day to receive an order through him, and God knows what order, too! That sort of thing has happened once before – and that's once too often. He understands this perfectly, never fear. I can't tell you more than this. Now go. You know what it is you have to do."

This encounter took place outside the town of Lubeck, on very open ground selected with special care in deference to the general sense of the cavalry division belonging to the army corps, that this time the two officers should meet on horseback. After all, this duel was a cavalry affair, and to persist in fighting on foot would look like a slight on one's own arm of the service. The seconds, startled by the unusual nature of the suggestion, hastened to refer to their principals. Captain Feraud jumped at it with savage alacrity. For some obscure reason, depending, no doubt, on his psychology, he imagined himself invincible on horseback. All alone within the four walls of his room he rubbed his hands exultingly. "Aha! my staff officer, I've got you now!"

Captain D'Hubert, on his side, after staring hard for a considerable time at his bothered seconds, shrugged his shoulders slightly. This affair had hopelessly and unreasonably complicated his existence for him. One absurdity more or less in the development did not matter. All absurdity was distasteful to him; but, urbane as ever, he produced a faintly ironic smile and said in his calm voice:

"It certainly will do away to some extent with the monotony of the thing."

But, left to himself, he sat down at a table and took his head into his hands. He had not spared himself of late, and the marshal had been working his aides-de-camp particularly hard. The last three weeks of campaigning in horrible weather had affected his health. When overtired he suffered from a stitch in his wounded side, and that uncomfortable sensation always depressed him. "It's that brute's doing," he thought bitterly.

The day before he had received a letter from home, announcing that his only sister was going to be married. He reflected that from the time she was sixteen, when he went away to garrison life in Strasburg, he had had but two short glimpses of her. They had been great friends and confidants; and now they were going to give her away to a man whom he did not know – a very worthy fellow, no doubt, but not half good enough for her. He would never see his old Léonie again. She had a capable little head and plenty of tact; she would know how to manage the fellow, to be sure. He was easy about her happiness, but he felt ousted from the first place in her affection which had been his ever since the girl could speak. And a melancholy regret of the days of his childhood settled upon Captain D'Hubert, third aide-de-camp to the Prince of Ponte-Corvo.

He pushed aside the letter of congratulation he had begun to write, as in duty bound but without pleasure. He took a fresh sheet of paper and wrote: "This is my last will and testament." And, looking at these words, he gave himself up to unpleasant reflection; a presentiment that he would never see the scenes of his childhood overcame Captain D'Hubert. He jumped up, pushing his chair back, yawned leisurely, which demonstrated to himself that he didn't care anything for presentiments, and, throwing himself on the bed, went to sleep. During the night he shivered from time to time without waking up. In the morning he rode out of town between his two seconds, talking of indifferent things and looking right and left with apparent detachment into the heavy morning mists, shrouding the flat green fields bordered by hedges. He leaped a ditch, and saw the forms of many mounted men moving in the low fog. "We are to fight before a gallery," he muttered bitterly.

His seconds were rather concerned at the state of the atmosphere, but presently a pale and sympathetic sun struggled above the vapors. Captain D'Hubert made out in the distance three horsemen riding a little apart; it was his adversary and his seconds. He drew his saber and assured himself that it was properly fastened to his wrist. And now the seconds, who had been standing in a close group with the heads of their horses together, separated at an easy canter, leaving a large, clear field between him and his adversary. Captain D'Hubert looked at the pale sun, at the dismal landscape, and the imbecility of the impending fight filled him with desolation. From a distant part of the field a stentorian voice shouted commands at proper intervals: *Au pas – Au trot – Chargez!* Presentiments of death don't come to a man for nothing he thought at the moment he put spurs to his horse.

And therefore nobody was more surprised than himself when, at the very first set-to, Captain Feraud laid himself open to a cut extending over the forehead, blinding him with blood, and ending the combat almost before it had fairly begun. The surprise of Captain Feraud might have been even greater. Captain D'Hubert, leaving him swearing horribly and reeling in the saddle between his two appalled friends, leaped the ditch again and trotted home with his two seconds, who seemed rather awestruck at the speedy issue of that encounter. In the evening, Captain D'Hubert finished the congratulatory letter on his sister's marriage.

He finished it late. It was a long letter. Captain D'Hubert gave reins to his fancy. He told his sister he would feel rather lonely after this great change in her life. But, he continued, "the day will come for me, too, to get married. In fact, I am thinking already of the time when there will be no one left to fight in Europe, and the epoch of wars will be over. I shall expect then to be within measurable distance of a marshal's baton and you will be an experienced married woman. You shall look out a nice wife for me. I will be moderately bald by then, and a little blasé; I will require a young girl – pretty, of course, and with a large fortune, you know, to help me close my glorious career with the splendor befitting my exalted rank." He ended with the information that he had just given a lesson to a worrying, quarrelsome fellow, who imagined he had a grievance against him. "But if you, in the depth of your province," he continued, "ever hear it said that your brother is of a quarrelsome disposition, don't you believe it on any account. There is no saying what gossip from the army may reach your innocent ears; whatever you hear, you may assure our father that your ever loving brother is not a duelist." Then Captain D'Hubert crumpled up the sheet of paper with the words, "This is my last will and testament," and threw it in the fire with a great laugh at himself. He didn't care a snap for what that lunatic fellow could do. He had suddenly acquired the conviction that this man was utterly powerless to affect his life in any sort of way, except, perhaps, in the way of putting a certain special excitement into the delightful gay intervals between the campaigns.

From this on there were, however, to be no peaceful intervals in the career of Captain D'Hubert. He saw the fields of Eylau and Friedland, marched and countermarched in the snow, the mud, and the dust of Polish plains, picking up distinction and advancement on all the roads of northeastern Europe. Meantime, Captain Feraud, dispatched southward with his regiment, made unsatisfactory war in Spain. It was only when the preparations for the Russian campaign began that he was ordered north again. He left the country of mantillas and oranges without regret.

The first signs of a not unbecoming baldness added to the lofty aspect of Colonel D'Hubert's forehead. This feature was no longer white and smooth as in the days of his youth, and the kindly open glance of his blue eyes had grown a little hard, as if from much peering through the smoke of battles. The ebony crop on Colonel Feraud's head, coarse and crinkly like a cap of horsehair, showed many silver threads about the temples. A detestable warfare of ambushes and inglorious surprises had not improved his temper. The beaklike curve of his nose was unpleasantly set off by deep folds on each side of his mouth. The round orbits of his eyes radiated fine wrinkles. More than ever he recalled an irritable and staring fowl – something like a cross between a parrot and an owl. He still manifested an outspoken dislike for "intriguing fellows." He seized every opportunity to state that he did not pick up his rank in the anterooms of marshals.

The unlucky persons, civil or military, who, with an intention of being pleasant, begged Colonel Feraud to tell them how he came by that very apparent scar on the forehead, were astonished to find themselves snubbed in various ways, some of which were simply rude and others mysteriously sardonic. Young officers were warned kindly by their more experienced comrades not to stare openly at the colonel's scar. But, indeed, an officer need have been very young in his profession not to have heard the legendary tale of that duel originating in some mysterious, unforgivable offence.

III

The retreat from Moscow submerged all private feelings in a sea of disaster and misery. Colonels without regiments, D'Hubert and Feraud carried the musket in the ranks of the sacred battalion – a battalion recruited from officers of all arms who had no longer any troops to lead.

In that battalion promoted colonels did duty as sergeants; the generals captained the companies; a marshal of France, Prince of the Empire, commanded the whole. All had provided themselves with muskets picked up on the road, and cartridges taken from the dead. In the general destruction of the bonds of discipline and duty holding together the companies, the battalions, the regiments, the brigades and divisions of an armed host, this body of men put their pride in preserving some semblance of order and formation. The only stragglers were those who fell out to give up to the frost their exhausted souls. They plodded on doggedly, stumbling over the corpses of men, the carcasses of horses, the fragments of gun-carriages, covered by the white winding-sheet of the great disaster. Their passage did not disturb the mortal silence of the plains, shining with a livid light under a sky the color of ashes. Whirlwinds of snow ran along the fields, broke against the dark column, rose in a turmoil of flying icicles, and subsided, disclosing it creeping on without the swing and rhythm of the military pace. They struggled onward, exchanging neither words nor looks – whole ranks marched, touching elbows, day after day, and never raising their eyes, as if lost in despairing reflections. On calm days, in the dumb black forests of pines the cracking of overloaded branches was the only sound. Often from daybreak to dusk no one spoke in the whole column. It was like a *macabre* march of struggling corpses towards a distant grave. Only an alarm of Cossacks could restore to their lackluster eyes a semblance of martial resolution. The battalion deployed, facing about, or formed square under the endless fluttering of snowflakes. A cloud of horsemen with fur caps on their heads, leveled long lances and yelled "Hurrah! Hurrah!" around their menacing immobility, whence, with muffled detonations, hundreds of dark-red flames darted through the air thick with falling snow. In a very few moments the horsemen would disappear, as if carried off yelling in the gale, and the battalion, standing still, alone in the blizzard, heard only the wind searching their very hearts. Then, with a cry or two of *"Vive l'Empereur!"* it would resume its march, leaving behind a few lifeless bodies lying huddled up, tiny dark specks on the white ground.

Though often marching in the ranks or skirmishing in the woods side by side, the two officers ignored each other; this not so much from inimical intention as from a very real indifference. All their store of moral energy was expended in resisting the terrific enmity of Nature and the crushing sense of irretrievable disaster.

Neither of them allowed himself to be crushed. To

the last they counted among the most active, the least demoralized of the battalion; their vigorous vitality invested them both with the appearance of an heroic pair in the eyes of their comrades. And they never exchanged more than a casual word or two, except one day when, skirmishing in front of the battalion against a worrying attack of cavalry, they found themselves cut off by a small party of Cossacks. A score of wild-looking, hairy horsemen rode to and fro, brandishing their lances in ominous silence. The two officers had no mind to lay down their arms, and Colonel Feraud suddenly spoke up in a hoarse, growling voice, bringing his firelock to the shoulder:

"You take the nearest brute, Colonel D'Hubert; I'll settle the next one. I am a better shot than you are."

Colonel D'Hubert only nodded over his leveled musket. Their shoulders were pressed against the trunk of a large tree; in front, deep snowdrifts protected them from a direct charge.

Two carefully aimed shots rang out in the frosty air, two Cossacks reeled in their saddles. The rest, not thinking the game good enough, closed round their wounded comrades and galloped away out of range. The two officers managed to rejoin their battalion, halted for the night. During that afternoon they had leaned upon each other more than once, and towards the last Colonel D'Hubert, whose long legs gave him an advantage in walking through soft snow, peremptorily took the musket from Colonel Feraud and carried it on his shoulder, using his own as a staff.

On the outskirts of a village, half-buried in the snow, an old wooden barn burned with a clear and immense flame. The sacred battalion of skeletons muffled in rags crowded greedily the windward side, stretching hundreds of numbed, bony hands to the blaze. Nobody had noted their approach. Before entering the circle of light playing on the multitude of sunken, glassy-eyed, starved faces, Colonel D'Hubert spoke in his turn:

"Here's your firelock, Colonel Feraud. I can walk better than you."

Colonel Feraud nodded, and pushed on towards the warmth of the fierce flames. Colonel D'Hubert was more deliberate, but not the less bent on getting a place in the front rank. Those they pushed aside tried to greet with a faint cheer the reappearance of the two indomitable companions in activity and endurance. Those manly qualities had never, perhaps, received a higher tribute than this feeble acclamation.

This is the faithful record of speeches exchanged during the retreat from Moscow by Colonels Feraud and D'Hubert. Colonel Feraud's taciturnity was the outcome of concentrated rage. Short, hairy, black-faced with layers of grime, and a thick sprouting of a wiry beard, a frost-bitten hand, wrapped in filthy rags, carried in a sling, he accused fate bitterly of unparalleled perfidy towards the sublime Man of Destiny. Colonel D'Hubert, his long moustache pendent in icicles on each side of his cracked blue lips, his eyelids inflamed with the glare of snows, the principal part of his costume consisting of a sheepskin coat looted with difficulty from the frozen corpse of a camp follower found in an abandoned cart, took a more thoughtful view of events. His regularly handsome features now reduced to mere bony fines and fleshless hollows, looked out of a woman's black velvet hood, over which was rammed forcibly a cocked hat picked up under the wheels of an empty army fourgon which must have contained at one time some general officer's luggage. The sheepskin coat being short for a man of his inches, ended very high up his elegant person, and the skin of his legs, blue with the cold, showed through the tatters of his nether garments. This, under the circumstances, provoked neither jeers nor pity. No one cared how the next man felt or looked. Colonel D'Hubert himself hardened to exposure, suffered mainly in his self-respect from the lamentable indecency of his costume. A thoughtless person may think that with a whole host of inanimate bodies bestrewing the path of retreat there could not have been much difficulty in supplying the deficiency. But the great majority of these bodies lay buried under the falls of snow, others had been already despoiled; and besides, to loot a pair of breeches from a frozen corpse is not so easy as it may appear to a mere theorist. It requires time. You must remain behind while your companions march on. And Colonel D'Hubert had his scruples as to falling out. They arose from a point of honor, and also a little from dread. Once he stepped aside he could not be sure of ever rejoining his battalion. And the enterprise demanded a physical effort from which his starved body shrank. The ghastly intimacy of a wrestling match with the frozen dead opposing the unyielding rigidity of iron to your violence was repugnant to the inborn delicacy of his feelings.

Luckily, one day grubbing in a mound of snow between the huts of a village in the hope of finding there a frozen potato or some vegetable garbage he could put between his long and shaky teeth, Colonel D'Hubert uncovered a couple of mats of the sort Russian peasants use to line the sides of their carts. These, shaken free of frozen snow, bent about his person and fastened solidly round his waist, made a bell-shaped nether garment, a sort of stiff petticoat, rendering Colonel D'Hubert a perfectly decent but a much more noticeable figure than before.

Thus accoutered he continued to retreat, never doubting of his personal escape but full of other misgivings. The early buoyancy of his belief in the future was destroyed. If the road of glory led through such unforeseen passages – he asked himself, for he was reflective, whether the guide was altogether trustworthy. And a patriotic sadness not unmingled with some personal concern, altogether unlike the unreasoning indignation against men and things nursed by Colonel Feraud, oppressed the equable spirits of Colonel D'Hubert. Recruiting his strength in a little German town for three weeks, he was surprised to discover within himself a love of repose. His returning vigor was strangely pacific in its aspirations. He meditated silently upon that bizarre change of mood. No doubt many of his brother officers of field rank had the same personal experience. But these were not the times to talk of it. In one of his letters home Colonel D'Hubert wrote: "All your plans, my dear Leonie, of marrying me to the charming girl you have discovered in your neighborhood, seem farther off than ever. Peace is not yet. Europe wants another lesson. It will be a hard task for us, but it will be done well, because the emperor is invincible."

Thus wrote Colonel D'Hubert from Pomerania to his married sister Léonie, settled in the south of France. And so far the sentiments expressed would not have been disowned by Colonel Feraud who wrote no letters to anybody; whose father had been in life an illiterate blacksmith; who had no sister or brother, and whom no one desired ardently to pair off for a life of peace with a charming young girl. But Colonel D'Hubert's letter contained also some philosophical generalities upon the uncertainty of all personal hopes if bound up entirely with the prestigious fortune of one incomparably great, it is true, yet still remaining but a man in his greatness. This sentiment would have appeared rank heresy to Colonel Feraud. Some melancholy forebodings of a military kind expressed cautiously would have been pronounced as nothing short of high treason by Colonel Feraud. But Léonie, the sister of Colonel D'Hubert, read them with positive satisfaction, and folding the letter thoughtfully remarked to herself that "Armand was likely to prove eventually a sensible fellow." Since her marriage into a Southern family she had become a convinced believer in the return of the legitimate king. Hopeful and anxious she offered prayers night and morning, and burned candles in churches for the safety and prosperity of her brother.

She had every reason to suppose that her prayers were heard. Colonel D'Hubert passed through Lutzen, Bautzen, and Leipzig, losing no limbs and acquiring additional reputation. Adapting his conduct to the needs of that desperate time, he had never voiced his misgivings. He concealed them under a cheerful courtesy of such pleasant character that people were inclined to ask themselves with wonder whether Colonel D'Hubert was aware of any disasters. Not only his manners but even his glances remained untroubled. The steady amenity of his blue eyes disconcerted all grumblers, silenced doleful remarks, and made even despair pause.

This bearing was remarked at last by the emperor himself, for Colonel D'Hubert, attached now to the Major-General's staff, came on several occasions under the imperial eye. But it exasperated the higher strung nature of Colonel Feraud. Passing through Magdeburg on service this last allowed himself, while seated gloomily at dinner with the *Commandant de Place,* to say of his lifelong adversary: "This man does not love the emperor," – and as his words were received in profound silence Colonel Feraud, troubled in his conscience at the atrocity of the aspersion, felt the need to back it up by a good argument. "I ought to know him," he said, adding some oaths. "One studies one's adversary. I have met him on the ground half a dozen times, as all the army knows. What more do you want? If that isn't opportunity enough for any fool to size up his man, may the devil take me if I can tell what is." And he looked around the table with somber obstinacy.

Later on, in Paris, while feverishly busy reorganizing his regiment, Colonel Feraud learned that Colonel D'Hubert had been made a general. He glared at his informant incredulously, then folded his arms and turned away muttering:

"Nothing surprises me on the part of that man."

And aloud he added, speaking over his shoulder: "You would greatly oblige me by telling General D'Hubert at the first opportunity that his advancement saves him for a time from a pretty hot encounter. I was only waiting for him to turn up here."

The other officer remonstrated.

"Could you think of it, Colonel Feraud! At this time when every life should be consecrated to the glory and safety of France!"

But the strain of unhappiness caused by military reverses had spoiled Colonel Feraud's character. Like many other men he was rendered wicked by misfortune.

"I cannot consider General D'Hubert's person of any account either for the glory or safety of France," he snapped viciously. "You don't pretend, perhaps, to know him better than I do – who have been with him half a dozen times on the ground – do you?"

His interlocutor, a young man, was silenced. Colonel Feraud walked up and down the room.

"This is not a time to mince matters," he said. "I can't believe that that man ever loved the emperor. He picked up his general's stars under the boots of Marshal Berthier. Very well. I'll get mine in another fashion, and then we shall settle this business which has been dragging on too long."

General D'Hubert, informed indirectly of Colonel Feraud's attitude, made a gesture as if to put aside an importunate person. His thoughts were solicited by graver cares. He had had no time to go and see his family. His sister, whose royalist hopes were rising higher every day, though proud of her brother, regretted his recent advancement in a measure, because it put on him a prominent mark of the usurper's favor which later on could have an adverse influence upon his career. He wrote to her that no one but an inveterate enemy could say he had got his promotion by favor. As to his career he assured her that he looked no farther forward into the future than the next battlefield.

Beginning the campaign of France in that state of mind, General D'Hubert was wounded on the second day of the battle under Laon. While being carried off the field he heard that Colonel Feraud, promoted that moment to general, had been sent to replace him in the command of his brigade. He cursed his luck impulsively, not being able, at the first glance, to discern all the advantages of a nasty wound. And yet it was by this heroic method that Providence was shaping his future. Traveling slowly south to his sister's country house, under the care of a trusty old servant, General D'Hubert was spared the humiliating contacts and the perplexities of conduct which assailed the men of the Napoleonic empire at the moment of its downfall. Lying in his bed with the windows of his room open wide to the sunshine of Provençe, he perceived at last the undisguised aspect of the blessing conveyed by that jagged fragment of a Prussian shell which, killing his horse and ripping open his thigh, saved him from an active conflict with his conscience. After fourteen years spent sword in hand in the saddle and strong in the sense of his duty done to the end, General D'Hubert found resignation an easy virtue. His sister was delighted with his reasonableness. "I leave myself altogether in your hands, my dear Léonie," he had said.

He was still laid up when, the credit of his brother-in-law's family being exerted on his behalf, he received from the Royal Government not only the confirmation of his rank but the assurance of being retained on the active list. To this was added an unlimited convalescent leave. The unfavorable opinion entertained of him in the more irreconcilable Bonapartist circles, though it rested on nothing more solid than the unsupported pronouncement of General Feraud, was directly responsible for General D'Hubert's retention on the active list. As to General Feraud, his rank was confirmed, too. It was more than he dared to expect, but Marshal Soult, then Minister of War to the restored king, was partial to officers who had served in Spain. Only not even the marshal's protection could secure for him active employment. He remained irreconcilable, idle and sinister, seeking in obscure restaurants the company of other half-pay officers, who cherished dingy but glorious old tricolor cockades in their breast pockets, and buttoned with the forbidden eagle buttons their shabby uniform, declaring themselves too poor to afford the expense of the prescribed change.

The triumphant return of the emperor, a historical fact as marvelous and incredible as the exploits of some mythological demigod, found General D'Hubert still quite unable to sit a horse. Neither could he walk very well. These disabilities, which his sister thought most lucky, helped her immensely to keep her brother out of all possible mischief. His frame of mind at that time, she noted with dismay, became very far from reasonable. That general officer, still menaced by the loss of a limb, was discovered one night in the stables of the château by a groom who, seeing a light, raised an alarm of thieves. His crutch was lying half buried in the straw of the litter, and he himself was hopping on one leg in a loose box around a snorting horse he was trying to saddle. Such were the effects of imperial magic upon an unenthusiastic temperament and a pondered mind. Beset, in the light of stable lanterns, by the tears, entreaties, indignation, remonstrances and reproaches of his family, he got out of the difficult situation by fainting away there and then in the arms of his nearest relatives, and was carried off to bed. Before he got out of it again the second reign of Napoleon, the Hundred Days of feverish agitation and supreme effort passed away like a terrifying dream. The tragic year 1815, begun in the trouble and unrest of consciences, was ending in vengeful proscriptions.

How General Feraud escaped the clutches of the Special Commission and the last offices of a firing squad, he never knew himself. It was partly due to the subordinate position he was assigned during the Hundred Days. He was not given active command but was kept busy at the cavalry depot in Paris, mounting and dispatching hastily drilled troopers into the field. Considering this task as unworthy of his abilities, he discharged it with no offensively noticeable zeal. But for the greater part he was saved from the excesses of royalist reaction by the interference of General D'Hubert.

This last, still on convalescent leave but able now to travel, had been dispatched by his sister to Paris to present himself to his legitimate sovereign. As no one in the capital could possibly know anything of the episode in the stable, he was received there with distinction. Military to the very bottom of his soul, the prospect of rising in his profession consoled him from finding himself the butt of Bonapartist malevolence which pursued him with a persistence he could not account for. All the rancor of that embittered and persecuted party pointed to him as the man who had *never* loved the emperor – a sort of monster essentially worse than a mere betrayer.

General D'Hubert shrugged his shoulders without anger at this ferocious prejudice. Rejected by his old friends and mistrusting profoundly the advances of royalist society, the young and handsome general (he was barely forty) adopted a manner of punctilious and cold courtesy which at the merest shadow of an intended slight passed easily into harsh haughtiness. Thus prepared, General D'Hubert went about his affairs in Paris feeling inwardly very happy with the peculiar uplifting happiness of a man very much in love. The charming girl looked out by his sister had come upon the scene and had conquered him in the thorough manner in which a young girl, by merely existing in his sight, can make a man of forty her own. They were going to be married as soon as General D'Hubert had obtained his official nomination to a promised command.

One afternoon, sitting on the *terrasse* of the Café Tortoni, General D'Hubert learned from the conversation of two strangers occupying a table near his own that General Feraud, included in the batch of superior officers arrested after the second return of the king, was in danger of passing before the Special Commission. Living all his spare moments, as is frequently the case with expectant lovers a day in advance of reality, as it were, and in a state of bestarred hallucination, it required nothing less than the name of his perpetual antagonist pronounced in a loud voice to call the youngest of Napoleon's generals away from the mental contemplation of his betrothed. He looked round. The strangers wore civilian clothes. Lean and weather-beaten, lolling back in their chairs, they looked at people with moody and defiant abstraction from under their hats pulled low over their eyes. It was not difficult to recognize them for two of the compulsorily retired officers of the Old Guard. As from bravado or carelessness they chose to speak in loud tones, General D'Hubert, who saw no reason why he should change his seat, heard every word. They did not seem to be the personal friends of General Feraud. His name came up with some others; and hearing it repeated General D'Hubert's tender anticipations of a domestic future adorned by a woman's grace were traversed by the harsh regret of that warlike past, of that one long, intoxicating clash of arms, unique in the magnitude of its glory and disaster – the marvelous work and the special possession of his own generation. He felt an irrational tenderness toward his old adversary, and appreciated emotionally the murderous absurdity their encounter had introduced into his life. It was like an additional pinch of spice in a hot dish. He remembered the flavor with sudden melancholy. He would never taste it again. It was all over. . . . "I fancy it was being left lying in the garden that had exasperated him so against me," he thought indulgently.

The two strangers at the next table had fallen silent upon the third mention of General Feraud's name. Presently, the oldest of the two, speaking in a bitter tone, affirmed that General Feraud's account was settled. And why? Simply because he was not like some big-wigs who loved only themselves. The royalists knew that they could never make anything of him. He loved the Other too well.

The Other was the man of St. Helena. The two officers nodded and touched glasses before they drank to an impossible return. Then the same who had spoken before remarked with a sardonic little laugh:

"His adversary showed more cleverness."

"What adversary?" asked the younger as if puzzled.

"Don't you know? They were two Hussars. At each promotion they fought a duel. Haven't you heard of the duel that is going on since 1801?"

His friend had heard of the duel, of course. Now he understood the allusion. General Baron D'Hubert would be able now to enjoy his fat king's favor in peace.

"Much good may it do to him," mumbled the elder. "They were both brave men. I never saw this D'Hubert – a sort of intriguing dandy, I understand. But I can well believe what I've heard Feraud say once of him – that he never loved the emperor."

They rose and went away.

General D'Hubert experienced the horror of a somnambulist who wakes up from a complacent dream of activity to find himself walking on a quagmire. A profound disgust of the ground on which he was making his way overcame him. Even the image of the charming girl was swept from his view in the flood of moral distress. Everything he had ever been or hoped to be would be lost in ignominy unless he could manage to save General Feraud from the fate which threatened so many braves. Under the impulse of this almost morbid need to attend to the safety of his adversary General D'Hubert worked so well with hands and feet (as the French saying is) that in less than twenty-four hours he found means of obtaining an extraordinary private audience from the Minister of Police.

General Baron D'Hubert was shown in suddenly without preliminaries. In the dusk of the minister's cabinet, behind the shadowy forms of writing desk, chairs, and tables, between two bunches of wax candles blazing in sconces, he beheld a figure in a splendid coat posturing before a tall mirror. The old *Conventional* Fouché, ex-senator of the empire, traitor to every man, every principle and motive of human conduct, Duke of Otranto, and the wily artisan of the Second Restoration, was trying the fit of a court suit, in which his young and accomplished *fiancée* had declared her wish to have his portrait painted on porcelain. It was a caprice, a charming fancy which the Minister of Police of the Second Restoration was anxious to gratify. For that man, often compared in wiliness of intellect to a fox but whose ethical side could be worthily symbolized by nothing less emphatic than a skunk, was as much possessed by his love as General D'Hubert himself.

Startled to be discovered thus by the blunder of a servant, he met this little vexation with the characteristic effrontery which had served his turn so well in the endless intrigues of his self-seeking career. Without altering his attitude a hair's breadth, one leg in a silk stocking advanced, his head twisted over his left shoulder, he called out calmly:

"This way, general. Pray approach. Well? I am all attention."

While General D'Hubert, as ill at ease as if one of his own little weaknesses had been exposed, presented his request as shortly as possible, the minister went on feeling the fit of his collar, settling the lapels before the glass or buckling his back in his efforts to behold the set of the gold-embroidered coat skirts behind. His still face, his attentive eyes, could not have expressed a more complete interest in those matters if he had been alone.

"Exclude from the operations of the Special Commission a certain Feraud, Gabriel Florian, General of Brigade of the promotion of 1814?" he repeated in a slightly wondering tone and then turned away from the glass. "Why exclude him precisely?"

"I am surprised that your Excellency, so competent

in the valuation of men of his time, should have thought it worth while to have that name put down on the list."

"A rabid Bonapartist."

"So is every grenadier and every trooper of the army, as your Excellency well knows. And the individuality of General Feraud can have no more weight than that of any casual grenadier. He is a man of no mental grasp, of no capacity whatever. It is inconceivable that he should ever have any influence."

"He has a well-hung tongue though," interjected Fouché.

"Noisy, I admit, but not dangerous."

"I will not dispute with you. I know next to nothing of him. Hardly his name in fact."

"And yet your Excellency had the presidency of the commission charged by the king to point out those who were to be tried," said General D'Hubert with an emphasis which did not miss the minister's ear.

"Yes, general," he said, walking away into the dark part of the vast room and throwing himself into a high-backed armchair whose overshadowed depth swallowed him up, all but the gleam of gold embroideries on the coat and the pallid patch of the face. "Yes, general. Take that chair there."

General D'Hubert sat down.

"Yes, general," continued the arch-master in the arts of intrigue and betrayal, whose duplicity as if at times intolerable to his self-knowledge worked itself off in bursts of cynical openness. "I did hurry on the formation of the proscribing commission and took its presidency. And do you know why? Simply from fear that if I did not take it quickly into my hands my own name would head the list of the proscribed. Such are the times in which we live. But I am minister of the king as yet, and I ask you plainly why I should take the name of this obscure Feraud off the list? You wonder how his name got there. Is it possible that you know men so little? My dear general, at the very first sitting of the commission names poured on us like rain off the tiles of the Tuileries. Names! We had our choice of thousands. How do you know that the name of this Feraud, whose life or death don't matter to France, does not keep out some other name. . . ?"

The voice out of the armchair stopped. General D'Hubert sat still, shadowy, and silent. Only his saber clinked slightly. The voice in the armchair began again. "And we must try to satisfy the exigencies of the allied sovereigns. The Prince de Talleyrand told me only yesterday that Nesselrode had informed him officially that his Majesty, the Emperor Alexander, was very disappointed at the small number of examples the government of the king intends to make – especially amongst military men. I tell you this confidentially."

"Upon my word," broke out General D'Hubert, speaking through his teeth, "if your Excellency deigns to favor me with anymore confidential information I don't know what I will do. It's enough to make one break one's sword over one's knee and fling the pieces . . ."

"What government do you imagine yourself to be serving?" interrupted the minister sharply. After a short pause the crestfallen voice of General D'Hubert answered:

"The government of France."

"That's paying your conscience off with mere words, general. The truth is that you are serving a government of returned exiles, of men who have been without country for twenty years. Of men also who have just got over a very bad and humiliating fright. . . . Have no illusions on that score."

The Duke of Otranto ceased. He had relieved himself, and had attained his object of stripping some self-respect off that man who had inconveniently discovered him posturing in a gold-embroidered court costume before a mirror. But they were a hotheaded lot in the army, and it occurred to him that it would be inconvenient if a well-disposed general officer, received by him on the recommendation of one of the princes, were to go and do something rashly scandalous directly after a private interview with the minister. In a changed voice he put a question to the point:

"Your relation – this Feraud?"

"No. No relation at all."

"Intimate friend?"

"Intimate . . . yes. There is between us an intimate connection of a nature which makes it a point of honor with me to try . . ."

The minister rang a bell without waiting for the end of the phrase. When the servant had gone, after bringing in a pair of heavy silver candelabra for the writing desk, the Duke of Otranto stood up, his breast glistening all over with gold in the strong light, and taking a piece of paper out of a drawer held it in his hand ostentatiously while he said with persuasive gentleness:

"You must not talk of breaking your sword across your knee, general. Perhaps you would never get another. The emperor shall not return this time. . . . *Diable d'homme!* There was just a moment here in Paris, soon after Waterloo, when he frightened me. It looked as though he were going to begin again. Luckily one never does begin again really. You must not think of breaking your sword, general."

General D'Hubert, his eyes fixed on the ground, made with his hand a hopeless gesture of renunciation. The Minister of Police turned his eyes away from him and began to scan deliberately the paper he had been holding up all the time.

"There are only twenty general officers to be brought before the Special Commission. Twenty. A round number. And let's see, Feraud. Ah, he's there! Gabriel Florian. *Parfaitement.* That's your man. Well, there will be only nineteen examples made now."

General D'Hubert stood up feeling as though he had gone through an infectious illness.

"I must beg your Excellency to keep my interference a profound secret. I attach the greatest importance to his never knowing . . ."

"Who is going to inform him I should like to know," said Fouché, raising his eyes curiously to General D'Hubert's white face. "Take one of these pens and run it through the name yourself. This is the only list in existence. If you are careful to take up enough ink no one will be able to tell even what was the name thus struck out. But, *par example,* I am not responsible for what Clarke will do with him. If he persist in being rabid he will be ordered by the Minster of War to reside in some provincial town under the supervision of the police."

A few days later General D'Hubert was saying to his sister after the first greetings had been got over:

"Ah, my dear Léonie! It seemed to me I couldn't get away from Paris quick enough."

"Effect of love," she suggested with a malicious smile.

"And horror," added General D'Hubert with profound seriousness. "I have nearly died there of . . . of nausea."

His face was contracted with disgust. And as his sister looked at him attentively he continued:

"I have had to see Fouché. I have had an audience. I have been in his cabinet. There remains with one, after the misfortune of having to breathe the air of the same room with that man, a sense of diminished dignity, the uneasy feeling of being not so clean after all as one hoped one was. . . . But you can't understand."

She nodded quickly several times. She understood very well on the contrary. She knew her brother thoroughly and liked him as he was. Moreover, the scorn and loathing of mankind were the lot of the Jacobin Fouché, who, exploiting for his own advantage every weakness, every virtue, every generous illusion of mankind, made dupes of his whole generation and died obscurely as Duke of Otranto.

"My dear Armand," she said compassionately, "what could you want from that man?"

"Nothing less than a life," answered General D'Hubert. "And I've got it. It had to be done. But I feel yet as if I could never forgive the necessity to the man I had to save."

General Feraud, totally unable as is the case with most men to comprehend what was happening to him, received the Minister of War's order to proceed at once to a small town of Central France with feelings whose natural expression consisted in a fierce rolling of the eye and savage grinding of the teeth. But he went. The bewilderment and awe at the passing away of the state of war – the only condition of society he had ever known – the prospect of a world at peace frightened him. He went away to his little town firmly persuaded that this could not last. There he was informed of his retirement from the army, and that his pension (calculated on the scale of a colonel's half-pay) was made dependent on the circumspection of his conduct and on the good reports of the police. No longer in the army! He felt suddenly a stranger to the earth like a disembodied spirit. It was impossible to exist. But at first he reacted from sheer incredulity. This could not be. It could not last. The heavens would fall presently.

He called upon thunder, earthquakes, natural cataclysms. But nothing happened. The leaden weight of an irremediable idleness descended upon General Feraud, who, having no resources within himself, sank into a state of awe-inspiring hebetude. He haunted the streets of the little town gazing before him with lack-luster eyes, disregarding the hats raised on his passage; and the people, nudging each other as he went by, said: "That's poor General Feraud. His heart is broken. Behold how he loved the emperor!"

The other living wreckage of Napoleonic tempest to be found in that quiet nook of France clustered round him infinitely respectful of that sorrow. He himself imagined his soul to be crushed by grief. He experienced quickly succeeding impulses to weep, to howl, to bite his fists till blood came, to lie for days on his bed with his head thrust under the pillow; but they arose from sheer *ennui,* from the anguish of an immense, indescribable, inconceivable boredom. Only his mental inability to grasp the hopeless nature of his case as a whole saved him from suicide. He never even thought of it once. He thought of nothing; but his appetite abandoned him, and the difficulty of expressing the overwhelming horror of his feelings (the most furious swearing could do no justice to it) induced gradually a habit of silence: – a sort of death to a Southern temperament.

Great therefore was the emotion amongst the *anciens militaires* frequenting a certain little café full of flies when one stuffy afternoon "that poor General Feraud" let out suddenly a volley of formidable curses.

He had been sitting quietly in his own privileged corner looking through the Paris gazettes with about as much interest as a condemned man on the eve of execution could be expected to show in the news of the day. A cluster of martial, bronzed faces, including one lacking an eye and another lacking the tip of a nose frost-bitten in Russia, surrounded him anxiously.

"What's the matter, general?"

General Feraud sat erect, holding the newspaper at arm's length in order to make out the small print better. He was reading very low to himself over again fragments of the intelligence which had caused what may be called his resurrection.

"We are informed . . . till now on sick leave . . . is to be called to the command of the 5th Cavalry Brigade in . . ."

He dropped the paper stonily, mumbled once more . . . "Called to the command" . . . and suddenly gave his forehead a mighty slap.

"I had almost forgotten him," he cried in a conscience-stricken tone.

A deep-chested veteran shouted across the café:

"Some new villainy of the government, general?"

"The villainies of these scoundrels," thundered General Feraud, "are innumerable. One more, one less. . . !" He lowered his tone. "But I will set good order to one of them at least."

He looked all round the faces. "There's a pomaded curled staff officer, the darling of some of the marshals who sold their father for a handful of English gold. He will find out presently that I am alive yet," he declared in a dogmatic tone. . . . "However, this is a private affair. An old affair of honor. Bah! Our honor does not matter. Here we are driven off with a split ear like a lot of cast troop horses – good only for a knacker's yard. Who cares for our honor now? But it would be like striking a blow for the emperor. . . . *Messieurs,* I require the assistance of two of you."

Every man moved forward. General Feraud, deeply touched by this demonstration, called with visible emotion upon the one-eyed veteran cuirassier and the officer of the *Chasseurs à cheval,* who had left the tip of his nose in Russia. He excused his choice to the others.

"A cavalry affair this – you know."

He was answered with a varied chorus of *"Parfaitement mon Général . . . C'est juste . . . Parbleu c'est connu . . ."* Everybody was satisfied. The three left the café together, followed by cries of *"Bonne chance."*

Outside they linked arms, the general in the middle. The three rusty cocked hats worn *en bataille,* with a sinister forward slant, barred the narrow street nearly right across. The overheated little town of grey stones and red tiles was drowsing away its provincial afternoon under a blue sky. Far off the loud blows of some coopers hooping a cask, reverberated regularly between the houses. The general dragged his left foot a little in the shade of the walls.

"That damned winter of 1813 got into my bones for good. Never mind. We must take pistols, that's all. A little lumbago. We must have pistols. He's sure game for my bag. My eyes are as keen as ever. Always were. You should have seen me picking off the dodging Cossacks with a beastly old infantry musket. I have a natural gift for firearms."

In this strain General Feraud ran on, holding up his head with owlish eyes and rapacious beak. A mere fighter all his life, a cavalry man, a *sabreur,* he conceived war with the utmost simplicity as in the main a massed lot of personal contests, a sort of gregarious dueling. And here he had on hand a war of his own. He revived. The shadow of peace had passed away from him like the shadow of death. It was a marvelous resurrection of the named Feraud, Gabriel Florian, *engagé volontaire* of 1793, general of 1814, buried without ceremony by means of a service order signed by the War Minister of the Second Restoration.

IV

No man succeeds in everything he undertakes. In that sense we are all failures. The great point is not to fail in ordering and sustaining the effort of our life. In this matter vanity is what leads us astray. It is our vanity which hurries us into situations from which we must come out damaged. Whereas pride is our safeguard by the reserve it imposes on the choice of our endeavor, as much as by the virtue of its sustaining power.

General D'Hubert was proud and reserved. He had not been damaged by casual love affairs successful or otherwise. In his war-scarred body his heart at forty remained unscratched. Entering with reserve into his sister's matrimonial plans, he felt himself falling irremediably in love as one falls off a roof. He was too proud to be frightened. Indeed, the sensation was too delightful to be alarming.

The inexperience of a man of forty is a much more serious thing than the inexperience of a youth of twenty, for it is not helped out by the rashness of hot blood. The girl was mysterious, as all young girls are, by the mere effect of their guarded ingenuity; and to him the mysteriousness of that young girl appeared exceptional and fascinating. But there was nothing mysterious about the arrangements of the match which Madame Léonie had arranged. There was nothing peculiar, either. It was a very appropriate match, commending itself extremely to the young lady's mother (her father was dead) and tolerable to the young lady's uncle – an old *émigré*, lately returned from Germany, and pervading cane in hand like a lean ghost of the *ancien régime* in a long-skirted brown coat and powdered hair, the garden walks of the young lady's ancestral home.

General D'Hubert was not the man to be satisfied merely with the girl and the fortune – when it came to the point. His pride – and pride aims always at true success – would be satisfied with nothing short of love. But as pride excludes vanity, he could not imagine any reason why this mysterious creature, with deep and candid eyes of a violet color, should have any feeling for him warmer than indifference. The young lady (her name was Adèle) baffled every attempt at a clear understanding on that point. It is true that the attempts were clumsy and timidly made, because by then General D'Hubert had become acutely aware of the number of his years, of his wounds, of his many moral imperfections, of his secret unworthiness – and had incidentally learned by experience the meaning of the word funk. As far as he could make it out she seemed to imply that with a perfect confidence in her mother's affection and sagacity she had no pronounced antipathy for the person of General D'Hubert; and that this was quite sufficient for a well-brought-up dutiful young lady to begin married life upon. This view hurt and tormented the pride of General D'Hubert. And yet, he asked himself with a sort of sweet despair, What more could he expect? She had a quiet and luminous forehead; her violet eyes laughed while the lines of her lips and chin remained composed in an admirable gravity. All this was set off by such a glorious mass of fair hair, by a complexion so marvelous, by such a grace of expression, that General D'Hubert really never found the opportunity to examine, with sufficient detachment, the lofty exigencies of his pride. In fact, he became shy of that line of inquiry, since it had led once or twice to a crisis of solitary passion in which it was borne upon him that he loved her enough to kill her rather than lose her. From such passages, not unknown to men of forty, he would come out broken, exhausted, remorseful, a little dismayed. He derived, however, considerable comfort from the quietist practice of sitting up now and then half the night by an open window, and meditating upon the wonder of her existence, like a believer lost in the mystic contemplation of his faith.

It must not be supposed that all these variations of his inward state were made manifest to the world. General D'Hubert found no difficulty in appearing wreathed in smiles: because, in fact, he was very happy. He followed the established rules of his condition, sending over flowers (from his sister's garden and hothouses) early every morning, and a little later following himself to have lunch with his intended, her mother, and her *émigré* uncle. The middle of the day was spent in strolling or sitting in the shade. A watchful deferential gallantry trembling on the verge of tenderness, was the note of their intercourse on his side – with a playful turn of the phrase concealing the profound trouble of his whole being caused by her inaccessible nearness. Late in the afternoon General D'Hubert walked home between the fields of vines, sometimes intensely miserable, sometimes supremely happy, sometimes pensively sad, but always feeling a special intensity of existence: that elation common to artists, poets, and lovers, to men haunted by a great passion, by a noble thought or a new vision of plastic beauty.

The outward world at that time did not exist with any special distinctness for General D'Hubert. One evening, however, crossing a ridge from which he could see both houses, General D'Hubert became aware of two figures far down the road. The day had been divine. The festal decoration of the inflamed sky cast a gentle glow on the sober tints of the southern land. The grey rocks, the brown fields, the purple undulating distances harmonized in luminous accord, exhaled already the scents of the evening. The two figures down the road presented themselves like two rigid and wooden silhouettes all black on the ribbon of white dust. General D'Hubert made out the long, straight-cut military *capotes*, buttoned closely right up to the black stocks, the cocked hats, the lean carven brown countenances – old soldiers – *vieilles moustaches!* The taller of the two had a black patch over one eye; the other's hard, dry countenance presented some bizarre disquieting peculiarity which, on nearer approach, proved to be the absence of the tip of the nose. Lifting their hands with one movement to salute the slightly lame civilian walking with a thick stick, they inquired for the house where the General Baron D'Hubert lived and what was the best way to get speech with him quietly.

"If you think this quiet enough," said General D'Hubert, looking round at the ripening vine-fields framed in purple lines and dominated by the nest of grey and drab walls of a village clustering around the top of a steep, conical hill, so that the blunt church tower seemed but the shape of a crowning rock – "if you think this quiet enough you can speak to him at once. And I beg you, comrades, to speak openly with perfect confidence."

They stepped back at this and raised again their hands to their hats with marked ceremoniousness. Then the one with the chipped nose, speaking for both, remarked that the matter was confidential enough and to be arranged discreetly. Their general quarters were in that village over there where the infernal clodhoppers – damn their false royalist hearts – looked remarkably cross-eyed at three unassuming military men. For the present he should only ask for the name of General D'Hubert's friends.

"What friends?" said the astonished General D'Hubert, completely off the track. "I am staying with my brother-in-law over there."

"Well, he will do for one," suggested the chipped veteran.

"We're the friends of General Feraud," interjected the other, who had kept silent till then, only glowering with his one eye at the man who had never loved the emperor. That was something to look at. For even the gold-laced Judases who had sold him to the English, the marshals and princes, had loved him at some time or other. But this man had *never* loved the emperor. General Feraud had said so distinctly.

General D'Hubert felt a sort of inward blow in his chest. For an infinitesimal fraction of a second it was as if the spinning of the earth had become perceptible with an awful, slight rustle in the eternal stillness of space. But that was the noise of the blood in his ears and passed off at once. Involuntarily he murmured:

"Feraud! I had forgotten his existence."

"He's existing at present, very uncomfortably it is true, in the infamous inn of that nest of savages up there," said the one-eyed cuirassier dryly. "We arrived in your parts an hour ago on post horses. He's awaiting our return with impatience. There is hurry, you know.

The general has broken the ministerial order of sojourn to obtain from you the satisfaction he's entitled to by the laws of honor, and naturally he's anxious to have it all over before the *gendarmerie* gets the scent."

The other elucidated the idea a little further.

"Get back on the quiet – you understand? Phitt! No one the wiser. We have broken out, too. Your friend the king would be glad to cut off our scurvy pittances at the first chance. It's a risk. But honor before everything."

General D'Hubert had recovered his power of speech.

"So you come like this along the road to invite me to a throat-cutting match with that – that . . ." A laughing sort of rage took possession of him.

"Ha! ha! ha! ha!"

His fists on his hips, he roared without restraint while they stood before him lank and straight, as unexpected as though they had been shot up with a snap through a trapdoor in the ground. Only four-and-twenty months ago the masters of Europe, they had already the air of antique ghosts, they seemed less substantial in their faded coats than their own narrow shadows falling so black across the white road – the military and grotesque shadows of twenty years of war and conquests. They had the outlandish appearance of two imperturbable bronzes of the religion of the sword. And General D'Hubert, also one of the ex-masters of Europe, laughed at these serious phantoms standing in his way.

Said one, indicating the laughing general with a jerk of the head:

"A merry companion that."

"There are some of us that haven't smiled from the day the Other went away," said his comrade.

A violent impulse to set upon and beat these unsubstantial wraiths to the ground frightened General D'Hubert. He ceased laughing suddenly. His urgent desire now was to get rid of them, to get them away from his sight quickly before he lost control of himself. He wondered at this fury he felt rising in his breast. But he had no time to look into that peculiarity just then.

"I understand your wish to be done with me as quickly as possible. Then why waste time in empty ceremonies. Do you see that wood there at the foot of that slope? Yes, the wood of pines. Let us meet there tomorrow at sunrise. I will bring with me my sword or my pistols or both if you like."

The seconds of General Feraud looked at each other.

"Pistols, general," said the cuirassier.

"So be it. *Au revoir* – tomorrow morning. Till then let me advise you to keep close if you don't want the *gendarmerie* making inquiries about you before dark. Strangers are rare in this part of the country."

They saluted in silence. General D'Hubert, turning his back on their retreating figures, stood still in the middle of the road for a long time, biting his lower lip and looking on the ground. Then he began to walk straight before him, thus retracing his steps till he found himself before the park gate of his intended's home. Motionless he stared through the bars at the front of the house gleaming clear beyond the thickets and trees. Footsteps were heard on the gravel, and presently a tall stooping shape emerged from the lateral alley following the inner side of the park wall.

Le Chevalier de Valmassigue, uncle of the adorable Adèle, ex-brigadier in the army of the princes, bookbinder in Altona, afterwards shoemaker (with a great reputation for elegance in the fit of ladies' shoes) in another small German town, wore silk stockings on his lean shanks, low shoes with silver buckles, a brocaded waistcoat. A long-skirted coat *à la Française* covered loosely his bowed back. A small three-cornered hat rested on a lot of powdered hair tied behind in a queue.

"Monsieur le Chevalier," called General D'Hubert softly.

"What? You again here, *mon ami?* Have you forgotten something?"

"By heavens! That's just it. I have forgotten something. I am come to tell you of it. No – outside. Behind this wall. It's too ghastly a thing to be let in at all where she lives."

The Chevalier came out at once with that benevolent resignation some old people display towards the fugue of youth. Older by a quarter of a century than General D'Hubert, he looked upon him in the secret of his heart as a rather troublesome youngster in love. He had heard his enigmatical words very well, but attached no undue importance to what a mere man of forty so hard hit was likely to do or say. The turn of mind of the generation of Frenchmen grown up during the years of his exile was almost unintelligible to him. Their sentiments appeared to him unduly violent, lacking fineness and measure, their language needlessly exaggerated. He joined the general on the road, and they made a few steps in silence, the general trying to master his agitation and get proper control of his voice.

"Chevalier, it is perfectly true. I forgot something. I forgot till half an hour ago that I had an urgent affair of honor on my hands. It's incredible but so it is!"

All was still for a moment. Then in the profound evening silence of the countryside the thin, aged voice of the Chevalier was heard trembling slightly.

"Monsieur! That's an indignity."

It was his first thought. The girl born during his exile, the posthumous daughter of his poor brother, murdered by a band of Jacobins, had grown since his return very dear to his old heart, which had been starving on mere memories of affection for so many years.

"It is an inconceivable thing – I say. A man settles such affairs before he thinks of asking for a young girl's hand. Why! If you had forgotten for ten days longer you would have been married before your memory returned to you. In my time men did not forget such things – nor yet what's due to the feelings of an innocent young woman. If I did not respect them myself I would qualify your conduct in a way which you would not like."

General D'Hubert relieved himself frankly by a groan.

"Don't let that consideration prevent you. You run no risk of offending her mortally."

But the old man paid no attention to this lover's nonsense. It's doubtful whether he even heard.

"What is it?" he asked. "What's the nature of . . ."

"Call it a youthful folly, *Monsieur le Chevalier.* An inconceivable, incredible result of . . ."

He stopped short. "He will never believe the story," he thought. "He will only think I am taking him for a fool and get offended." General D'Hubert spoke up again. "Yes, originating in youthful folly it has become . . ."

The Chevalier interrupted. "Well then it must be arranged."

"Arranged."

"Yes. No matter what it may cost your *amour propre.* You should have remembered you were engaged. You forgot that, too, I suppose. And then you go and forget your quarrel. It's the most revolting exhibition of levity I ever heard of."

"Good heavens, Chevalier! You don't imagine I have been picking up that quarrel last time I was in Paris or anything of the sort. Do you?"

"Eh? What matters the precise date of your insane conduct!" exclaimed the Chevalier testily. "The principal thing is to arrange it . . ."

Noticing General D'Hubert getting restive and trying to place a word, the old *émigré* raised his arm and added with dignity:

"I've been a soldier, too. I would never dare to suggest a doubtful step to the man whose name my niece is to bear. I tell you that *entre gallants hommes* an affair can be always arranged."

"But, *saperlotte, Monsieur le Chevalier,* it's fifteen or sixteen years ago. I was a lieutenant of Hussars then."

The old Chevalier seemed confounded by the vehemently despairing tone of this information.

"You were a lieutenant of Hussars sixteen years ago?" he mumbled in a dazed manner.

"Why, yes! You did not suppose I was made a general in my cradle like a royal prince."

In the deepening purple twilight of the fields, spread with vine leaves, backed by a low band of somber crimson in the west, the voice of the old ex-officer in the army of the princes sounded collected, punctiliously civil.

"Do I dream? Is this a pleasantry? Or do you mean me to understand that you have been hatching an affair of honor for sixteen years?"

"It has clung to me for that length of time. That is my precise meaning. The quarrel itself is not to be explained easily. We have been on the ground several times during that time of course."

"What manners! What horrible perversion of manliness! Nothing can account for such inhumanity but the sanguinary madness of the Revolution which has tainted a whole generation," mused the returned *émigré* in a low tone. "Who is your adversary?" he asked a little louder.

"What? My adversary! His name is Feraud." Shadowy in his *tricorne* and old-fashioned clothes like a bowed thin ghost of the *ancien régime* the Chevalier voiced a ghostly memory.

"I can remember the feud about little Sophie Derval between Monsieur de Brissac, captain in the Bodyguards and d'Anjorrant. Not the pockmarked one. The other. The Beau d'Anjorrant as they called him. They met three times in eighteen months in a most gallant manner. It was the fault of that little Sophie, too, who *would* keep on playing . . ."

"This is nothing of the kind," interrupted General D'Hubert. He laughed a little sardonically. "Not at all so simple," he added. "Nor yet half so reasonable," he finished inaudibly between his teeth and ground them with rage.

After this sound nothing troubled the silence for a long time till the Chevalier asked without animation:

"What is he – this Feraud?"

"Lieutenant of Hussars, too – I mean he's a general. A Gasçon. Son of a blacksmith, I believe."

"There! I thought so. That Bonaparte had a special predilection for the *canaille.* I don't mean this for you, D'Hubert. You are one of us, though you have served this usurper who . . ."

"Let's leave him out of this," broke in General D'Hubert.

The Chevalier shrugged his peaked shoulders.

"A Feraud of sorts. Offspring of a blacksmith and some village troll. . . . See what comes of mixing yourself up with that sort of people."

"You have made shoes yourself, Chevalier."

"Yes. But I am not the son of a shoemaker. Neither are you, Monsieur D'Hubert. You and I have something that your Bonaparte's, princes, dukes, and marshals have not because there's no power on earth that could give it to them," retorted the *émigré,* with the rising animation of a man who has got hold of a hopeful argument. "Those people don't exist – all these Ferauds. Feraud! What is Feraud? A *va-nu-pieds* disguised into a general by a Corsican adventurer masquerading as an emperor. There is no earthly reason for a D'Hubert to *s'encanailler* by a duel with a person of that sort. You can make your excuses to him perfectly well. And if the *manant* takes it into his head to decline them you may simply refuse to meet him." "You say I may do that?" "Yes. With the clearest conscience." "*Monsieur le Chevalier!* To what do you think you have returned from your emigration?"

This was said in such a startling tone that the old exile raised sharply his bowed head, glimmering silvery white under the points of the little *tricorne.* For a long time he made no sound.

"God knows!" he said at last, pointing with a slow and grave gesture at a tall roadside cross mounted on a block of stone and stretching its arms of forged stone all black against the darkening red band in the sky. "God knows! If it were not for this emblem, which I remember seeing in this spot as a child, I would wonder to what we, who have remained faithful to our God and our king, have returned. The very voices of the people have changed."

"Yes, it is a changed France," said General D'Hubert. He had regained his calm. His tone was slightly ironic. "Therefore, I cannot take your advice. Besides, how is one to refuse to be bitten by a dog that means to bite? It's impracticable. Take my word for it. He isn't a man to be stopped by apologies or refusals. But there are other ways. I could, for instance, send a mounted messenger with a word to the brigadier of the *gendarmerie* in Senlac. These fellows are liable to arrest on my simple order. It would make some talk in the army, both the organized and the disbanded. Especially the disbanded. All *canaille.* All my comrades once – the companions in arms of Armand D'Hubert. But what need a D'Hubert care what people who don't exist may think? Or better still, I might get my brother-in-law to send for the mayor of the village and give him a hint. No more would be needed to get the three 'brigands' set upon with flails and pitchforks and hunted into some nice deep wet ditch. And nobody the wiser! It has been done only ten miles from here to three poor devils of the disbanded Red Lancers of the Guard going to their homes. What says your conscience, Chevalier? Can a D'Hubert do that thing to three men who do not exist?"

A few stars had come out on the blue obscurity, clear as crystal, of the sky. The dry, thin voice of the Chevalier spoke harshly.

"Why are you telling me all this?"

The general seized a withered, frail old hand with a strong grip.

"Because I owe you my fullest confidence. Who could tell Adèle but you? You understand why I dare not trust my brother-in-law nor yet my own sister. Chevalier! I have been so near doing these things that I tremble yet. You don't know how terrible this duel appears to me. And there's no escape from it."

He murmured after a pause, "It's a fatality," dropped the Chevalier's passive hand, and said in his ordinary conversational voice:

"I shall have to go without seconds. If it is my lot to remain on the ground, you at least will know all that can be made known of this affair."

The shadowy ghost of the *ancien régime* seemed to have become more bowed during the conversation.

"How am I to keep an indifferent face this evening

before those two women?" he groaned. "General! I find it very difficult to forgive you."

General D'Hubert made no answer.

"Is your cause good at least?"

"I am innocent."

This time he seized the Chevalier's ghostly arm above the elbow, gave it a mighty squeeze.

"I must kill him," he hissed, and opening his hand strode away down the road.

The delicate attentions of his adoring sister had secured for the general perfect liberty of movement in the house where he was a guest. He had even his own entrance through a small door in one corner of the orangery. Thus he was not exposed that evening to the necessity of dissembling his agitation before the calm ignorance of the other inmates. He was glad of it. It seemed to him that if he had to open his lips, he would break out into horrible imprecation, start breaking furniture, smashing china and glasses. From the moment he opened the private door, and while ascending the twenty-eight steps of winding staircase, giving access to the corridor on which his room opened, he went through a horrible and humiliating scene in which an infuriated madman, with bloodshot eyes and a foaming mouth, played inconceivable havoc with everything inanimate that may be found in a well-appointed dining room. When he opened the door of his apartment the fit was over, and his bodily fatigue was so great that he had to catch at the backs of the chairs as he crossed the room to reach a low and broad divan on which he let himself fall heavily. His moral prostration was still greater. That brutality of feeling, which he had known only when charging saber in hand, amazed this man of forty, who did not recognize in it the instinctive fury of his menaced passion. It was the revolt of jeopardized desire. In his mental and bodily exhaustion it got cleared, fined down, purified into a sentiment of melancholy despair at having, perhaps, to die before he had taught this beautiful girl to love him.

On that night General D'Hubert, either stretched on his back with his hands over his eyes or lying on his breast, with his face buried in a cushion, made the full pilgrimage of emotions. Nauseating disgust at the absurdity of the situation, dread of the fate that could play such a vile trick on a man, awe at the remote consequences of an apparently insignificant and ridiculous event in his past, doubt of his own fitness to conduct his existence and mistrust of his best sentiments – for what the devil did he want to go to Fouché for? – he knew them all in turn. "I am an idiot, neither more nor less," he thought. "A sensitive idiot. Because I overheard two men talk in a café . . . I am an idiot afraid of lies – whereas in life it is only truth that matters."

Several times he got up, and walking about in his socks, so as not to be heard by anybody downstairs, drank all the water he could find in the dark. And he tasted the torments of jealousy, too. She would marry somebody else. His very soul writhed. The tenacity of that Feraud, the awful persistence of that imbecile brute came to him with the tremendous force of a relentless fatality. General D'Hubert trembled as he put down the empty water ewer. "He will have me," he thought. General D'Hubert was tasting every emotion that life has to give. He had in his dry mouth the faint, sickly flavor of fear, not the honorable fear of a young girl's candid and amused glance, but the fear of death and the honorable man's fear of cowardice.

But if true courage consists in going out to meet an odious danger from which our body, soul and heart recoil together General D'Hubert had the opportunity to practice it for the first time in his life. He had charged exultingly at batteries and infantry squares and ridden with messages through a hail of bullets without thinking anything about it. His business now was to sneak out unheard, at break of day, to an obscure and revolting death. General D'Hubert never hesitated. He carried two pistols in a leather bag which he slung over his shoulder. Before he had crossed the garden his mouth was dry again. He picked two oranges. It was only after shutting the gate after him that he felt a slight faintness.

He stepped out disregarding it, and after going a few yards regained the command of his legs. He sucked an orange as he walked. It was a colorless and pellucid dawn. The wood of pines detached its columns of brown trunks and its dark-green canopy very clearly against the rocks of the grey hillside behind. He kept his eyes fixed on it steadily. That temperamental, good-humored coolness in the face of danger, which made him an officer liked by his men and appreciated by his superiors, was gradually asserting itself. It was like going into battle. Arriving at the edge of the wood he sat down on a boulder, holding the other orange in his hand, and thought that he had come ridiculously early on the ground. Before very long, however, he heard the swishing of bushes, footsteps on the hard ground, and the sounds of a disjointed loud conversation. A voice somewhere behind him said boastfully, "He's game for my bag."

He thought to himself, "Here they are. What's this about game? Are they talking of me?" And becoming aware of the orange in his hand he thought further, "These are very good oranges. Leonie's own tree. I may just as well eat this orange instead of flinging it away."

Emerging from a tangle of rocks and bushes, General Feraud and his seconds discovered General D'Hubert engaged in peeling the orange. They stood still waiting till he looked up. Then the seconds raised their hats, and General Feraud, putting his hands behind his back, walked aside a little way.

"I am compelled to ask one of you, messieurs, to act for me. I have brought no friends. Will you?"

The one-eyed cuirassier said judicially:

"That cannot be refused."

The other veteran remarked:

"It's awkward all the same."

"Owing to the state of the people's minds in this part of the country there was no one I could trust with the object of your presence here," explained General D'Hubert urbanely. They saluted, looked round, and remarked both together:

"Poor ground."

"It's unfit."

"Why bother about ground, measurements, and so on. Let us simplify matters. Load the two pairs of pistols. I will take those of General Feraud and let him take mine. Or, better still, let us take a mixed pair. One of each pair. Then we will go into the wood while you remain outside. We did not come here for ceremonies, but for war. War to the death. Any ground is good enough for that. If I fall you must leave me where I lie and clear out. It wouldn't be healthy for you to be found hanging about here after that."

It appeared after a short parley that General Feraud was willing to accept these conditions. While the seconds were loading the pistols he could be heard whistling, and was seen to rub his hands with an air of perfect contentment. He flung off his coat briskly, and General D'Hubert took off his own and folded it carefully on a stone.

"Suppose you take your principal to the other side of the wood and let him enter exactly in ten minutes from now," suggested General D'Hubert calmly, but feeling as if he were giving directions for his own execution. This, however, was his last moment of weakness.

"Wait! Let us compare watches first."

He pulled out his own. The officer with the chipped nose went over to borrow the watch of General Feraud. They bent their heads over them for a time.

"That's it. At four minutes to five by yours. Seven to, by mine."

It was the cuirassier who remained by the side of General D'Hubert, keeping his one eye fixed immovably on the white face of the watch he held in the palm of his hand. He opened his mouth wide, waiting for the beat of the last second, long before he snapped out the word:

"Avancez!"

General D'Hubert moved on, passing from the glaring sunshine of the Provençal morning into the cool and aromatic shade of the pines. The ground was clear between the reddish trunks, whose multitude, leaning at slightly different angles, confused his eye at first. It was like going into battle. The commanding quality of confidence in himself woke up in his breast. He was all to his affair. The problem was how to kill his adversary. Nothing short of that would free him from this imbecile nightmare. "It's no use wounding that brute," he thought. He was known as a resourceful officer. His comrades, years ago, used to call him "the strategist." And it was a fact that he could think in the presence of the enemy, whereas Feraud had been always a mere fighter. But a dead shot, unluckily.

"I must draw his fire at the greatest possible range," said General D'Hubert to himself.

At that moment he saw something white moving far off between the trees. The shirt of his adversary. He stepped out at once between the trunks exposing himself freely, then quick as lightning leaped back. It had been a risky move, but it succeeded in its object. Almost simultaneously with the pop of a shot a small piece of bark chipped off by the bullet stung his ear painfully.

And now General Feraud, with one shot expended, was getting cautious. Peeping round his sheltering tree, General D'Hubert could not see him at all. This ignorance of his adversary's whereabouts carried with it a sense of insecurity. General D'Hubert felt himself exposed on his flanks and rear. Again something white fluttered in his sight. Ha! The enemy was still on his front then. He had feared a turning movement. But, apparently, General Feraud was not thinking of it. General D'Hubert saw him pass without special haste from one tree to another in the straight line of approach. With great firmness of mind General D'Hubert stayed his hand. Too far yet. He knew he was no marksman. His must be a waiting game – to kill.

He sank down to the ground wishing to take advantage of the greater thickness of the trunk. Extended at full length, head on to his enemy, he kept his person completely protected. Exposing himself would not do now because the other was too near by this time. A conviction that Feraud would presently do something rash was like balm to General D'Hubert's soul. But to keep his chin raised off the ground was irksome, and not much use either. He peeped round, exposing a fraction of his head, with dread but really with little risk. His enemy, as a matter of fact, did not expect to see anything of him so low down as that. General D'Hubert caught a fleeting view of General Feraud shifting trees again with deliberate caution. "He despises my shooting," he thought, with that insight into the mind of his antagonist which is of such great help in winning battles. It confirmed him in his tactics of immobility. "Ah! if I only could watch my rear as well as my front!" he thought, longing for the impossible.

It required some fortitude to lay his pistols down. But on a sudden impulse General D'Hubert did this very gently – one on each side. He had been always looked upon as a bit of a dandy, because he used to shave and put on a clean shirt on the days of battle. As a matter of fact he had been always very careful of his personal appearance. In a man of nearly forty, in love with a young and charming girl, this praiseworthy self-respect may run to such little weaknesses as, for instance, being provided with an elegant leather folding case containing a small ivory comb and fitted with a piece of looking-glass on the outside. General D'Hubert, his hands being free, felt in his breeches pockets for that implement of innocent vanity, excusable in the possessor of long silky moustaches. He drew it out, and then, with the utmost coolness and promptitude, turned himself over on his back. In this new attitude, his head raised a little, holding the looking-glass in one hand just clear of his tree, he squinted into it with one eye while the other kept a direct watch on the rear of his position. Thus was proved Napoleon's saying, that for a French soldier the word impossible does not exist. He had the right tree nearly filling the field of his little mirror.

"If he moves from there," he said to himself exultingly, "I am bound to see his legs. And in any case he can't come upon me unawares."

And sure enough he saw the boots of General Feraud flash in and out, eclipsing for an instant everything else reflected in the little mirror. He shifted its position accordingly. But having to form his judgment of the change from that indirect view, he did not realize that his own feet and a portion of his legs were now in plain and startling view of General Feraud.

General Feraud had been getting gradually impressed by the amazing closeness with which his enemy had been keeping cover. He had spotted the right tree with bloodthirsty precision. He was absolutely certain of it. And yet he had not been able to sight as much as the tip of an ear. As he had been looking for it at the level of about five feet ten inches it was no great wonder – but it seemed very wonderful to General Feraud.

The first view of these feet and legs determined a rush of blood to his head. He literally staggered behind his tree, and had to steady himself with his hand. The other was lying on the ground – on the ground! Perfectly still, too! Exposed! What did it mean. . . ? The notion that he had knocked his adversary over at the first shot then entered General Feraud's head. Once there, it grew with every second of attentive gazing, overshadowing every other supposition – irresistible – triumphant – ferocious.

"What an ass I was to think I could have missed him!" he said to himself. "He was exposed *en plein* – the fool – for quite a couple of seconds."

And the general gazed at the motionless limbs, the last vestiges of surprise fading before an unbounded admiration of his skill.

"Turned up his toes! By the god of war that was a shot!" he continued mentally. "Got it through the head just where I aimed, staggered behind that tree, rolled over on his back and died."

And he stared. He stared, forgetting to move, almost awed, almost sorry. But for nothing in the world would he have had it undone. Such a shot! Such a shot! Rolled over on his back, and died!

For it was this helpless position, lying on the back, that shouted its sinister evidence at General Feraud. He could not possibly imagine that it might have been deliberately assumed by a living man. It was inconceivable. It was beyond the range of sane supposition. There was no possibility to guess the reason for it. And it must be said that General D'Hubert's turned-up feet looked thoroughly dead. General Feraud expanded his lungs for a stentorian shout to his seconds, but from what he felt to be an excessive scrupulousness, refrained for a while.

"I will just go and see first whether he breathes yet," he mumbled to himself, stepping out from behind his tree. This was immediately perceived by the resourceful General D'Hubert. He concluded it to be another shift. When he lost the boots out of the field of the mirror, he became uneasy. General Feraud had only stepped a little out of the line, but his adversary could not possibly have supposed him walking up with perfect unconcern. General D'Hubert, beginning to wonder where the other had dodged to, was come upon so suddenly that the first warning he had of his danger consisted in the long, early-morning shadow of his enemy falling aslant on his outstretched legs. He had not even heard a footfall on the soft ground between the trees!

It was too much even for his coolness. He jumped up instinctively, leaving the pistols on the ground. The irresistible instinct of most people (unless totally paralyzed by discomfiture) would have been to stoop – exposing themselves to the risk of being shot down in that position. Instinct, of course, is irreflective. It is its very definition. But it may be an inquiry worth pursuing, whether in reflective mankind the mechanical promptings of instinct are not affected by the customary mode of thought. Years ago, in his young days, Armand D'Hubert, the reflective promising officer, had emitted the opinion that in warfare one should "never cast back on the lines of a mistake." This idea afterward restated, defended, developed in many discussions, had settled into one of the stock notions of his brain, became a part of his mental individuality. And whether it had gone so inconceivably deep as to affect the dictates of his instinct, or simply because, as he himself declared, he was "too scared to remember the confounded pistols," the fact is that General D'Hubert never attempted to stoop for them. Instead of going back on his mistake, he seized the rough trunk with both hands and swung himself behind it with such impetuosity that going right round in the very flash and report of a pistol shot, he reappeared on the other side of the tree face to face with General Feraud, who, completely unstrung by such a show of agility on the part of a dead man, was trembling yet. A very faint mist of smoke hung before his face which had an extraordinary aspect as if the lower jaw had come unhinged.

"Not missed!" he croaked hoarsely from the depths of a dry throat.

This sinister sound loosened the spell which had fallen on General D'Hubert's senses.

"Yes, missed – a *bout portant*" he heard himself saying exultingly almost before he had recovered the full command of his faculties. The revulsion of feeling was accompanied by a gust of homicidal fury resuming in its violence the accumulated resentment of a lifetime. For years General D'Hubert had been exasperated and humiliated by an atrocious absurdity imposed upon him by that man's savage caprice. Besides, General D'Hubert had been in this last instance too unwilling to confront death for the reaction of his anguish not to take the shape of a desire to kill.

"And I have my two shots to fire yet," he added pitilessly.

General Feraud snapped his teeth, and his face assumed an irate, undaunted expression.

"Go on," he growled.

These would have been his last words on earth if General D'Hubert had been holding the pistols in his hand. But the pistols were lying on the ground at the foot of a tall pine. General D'Hubert had the second's leisure necessary to remember that he had dreaded death not as a man but as a lover, not as a danger but as a rival – not as a foe to life but as an obstacle to marriage. And, behold, there was the rival defeated! Miserably defeated-crushed – done for!

He picked up the weapons mechanically, and instead of firing them into General Feraud's breast, gave expression to the thought uppermost in his mind.

"You will fight no more duels now."

His tone of leisurely, ineffable satisfaction was too much for General Feraud's stoicism.

"Don't dawdle then, damn you for a cold-blooded staff-coxcomb!" he roared out suddenly out of an impassive face held erect on a rigid body.

General D'Hubert uncocked the pistols carefully. This proceeding was observed with a sort of gloomy astonishment by the other general.

"You missed me twice," he began coolly, shifting both pistols to one hand. "The last time within a foot or so. By every rule of single combat your life belongs to me. That does not mean that I want to take it now."

"I have no use for your forbearance," muttered General Feraud savagely.

"Allow me to point out that this is no concern of mine," said General D'Hubert, whose every word was dictated by a consummate delicacy of feeling. In anger, he could have killed that man, but in cold blood, he recoiled from humiliating this unreasonable being – a fellow soldier of the Grand Armée, his companion in the wonders and terrors of the military epic. "You don't set up the pretension of dictating to me what I am to do with what is my own."

General Feraud looked startled. And the other continued:

"You've forced me on a point of honor to keep my life at your disposal, as it were, for fifteen years. Very well. Now that the matter is decided to my advantage, I am going to do what I like with your life on the same principle. You shall keep it at my disposal as long as I choose. Neither more nor less. You are on your honor."

"I am! But *sacrebleu!* This is an absurd position for a general of the empire to be placed in," cried General Feraud, in the accents of profound and dismayed conviction. "It means for me to be sitting all the rest of my life with a loaded pistol in a drawer waiting for your word. It's . . . it's idiotic. I shall be an object of . . . of . . . derision."

"Absurd. . . ? Idiotic? Do you think so?" queried argumentatively General D'Hubert with sly gravity. "Perhaps. But I don't see how that can be helped. However, I am not likely to talk at large of this adventure. Nobody need ever know anything about it. Just as no one to this day, I believe, knows the origin of our quarrel. . . . Not a word more," he added hastily. "I can't really discuss this question with a man who, as far as I am concerned, does not exist."

When the duelists came out into the open, General Feraud walking a little behind and rather with the air of walking in a trance, the two seconds hurried towards them each from his station at the edge of the wood. General D'Hubert addressed them, speaking loud and distinctly:

"Messieurs! I make it a point of declaring to you solemnly in the presence of General Feraud that our difference is at last settled for good. You may inform all the world of that fact."

"A reconciliation after all!" they exclaimed together.

"Reconciliation? Not that exactly. It is something much more binding. Is it not so, general?"

General Feraud only lowered his head in sign of assent. The two veterans looked at each other. Later in the day when they found themselves alone, out of their moody friend's earshot, the cuirassier remarked suddenly:

"Generally speaking, I can see with my one eye as far or even a little farther than most people. But this beats me. He won't say anything."

"In this affair of honor I understand there has been from first to last always something that no one in the army could quite make out," declared the chasseur with the imperfect nose. "In mystery it began, in mystery it went on, and in mystery it is to end apparently. . . ."

General D'Hubert walked home with long, hasty strides, by no means uplifted by a sense of triumph. He had conquered, but it did not seem to him he had gained very much by his conquest. The night before he had grudged the risk of his life which appeared to him magnificent, worthy of preservation as an opportunity to win a girl's love. He had even moments when by a marvelous illusion this love seemed to him already his and his threatened life a still more magnificent opportunity of devotion. Now that his life was safe it had suddenly lost it special magnificence. It wore instead a specially alarming aspect as a snare for the exposure of unworthiness. As to the marvelous illusion of conquered love that had visited him for a moment in the agitated watches of the night which might have been his last on earth, he comprehended now its true nature. It had been merely a paroxysm of delirious conceit. Thus to this man sobered by the victorious issue of a duel, life appeared robbed of much of its charm simply because it was no longer menaced.

Approaching the house from the back through the orchard and the kitchen gardens, he could not notice the agitation which reigned in front. He never met a single soul. Only upstairs, while walking softly along the corridor, he became aware that the house was awake and much more noisy than usual. Names of servants were being called out down below in a confused noise of coming and going. He noticed with some concern that the door of his own room stood ajar, though the shutters had not been opened yet. He had hoped that his early excursion would have passed unperceived. He expected to find some servant just gone in; but the sunshine filtering through the usual cracks enabled him to see lying on the low divan something bulky which had the appearance of two women clasped in each other's arms. Tearful and consolatory murmurs issued mysteriously from that appearance. General D'Hubert pulled open the nearest pair of shutters violently. One of the women then jumped up. It was his sister. She stood for a moment with her hair hanging down and her arms raised straight up above her head, and then flung herself with a stifled cry into his arms. He returned her embrace, trying at the same time to disengage himself from it. The other woman had not risen. She seemed, on the contrary, to cling closer to the divan, hiding her face in the cushions. Her hair was also loose; it was admirably fair. General D'Hubert recognized it with staggering emotion. Mlle. de Valmassigue! Adèle! In distress!

He became greatly alarmed and got rid of his sister's hug definitely. Madame Léonie then extended her shapely bare arm out of her peignoir, pointing dramatically at the divan:

"This poor terrified child has rushed here two miles from home on foot – running all the way."

"What on earth has happened?" asked General

D'Hubert in a low, agitated voice. But Madame Léonie was speaking loudly.

"She rang the great bell at the gate and roused all the household – we were all asleep yet. You may imagine what a terrible shock. . . . Adèle, my dear child, sit up."

General D'Hubert's expression was not that of a man who imagines with facility. He did, however, fish out of chaos the notion that his prospective mother-in-law had died suddenly, but only to dismiss it at once. He could not conceive the nature of the event, of the catastrophe which could induce Mlle, de Valmassigue living in a house full of servants, to bring the news over the fields herself, two miles, running all the way.

"But why are you in this room?" he whispered, full of awe.

"Of course I ran up to see and this child . . . I did not notice it – she followed me. It's that absurd Chevalier," went on Madame Léonie, looking towards the divan. . . . "Her hair's come down. You may imagine she did not stop to call her maid to dress it before she started. . . . Adèle, my dear, sit up. . . . He blurted it all out to her at half-past four in the morning. She woke up early, and opened her shutters, to breathe the fresh air, and saw him sitting collapsed on a garden bench at the end of the great alley. At that hour – you may imagine! And the evening before he had declared himself indisposed. She just hurried on some clothes and flew down to him. One would be anxious for less. He loves her, but not very intelligently. He had been up all night, fully dressed, the poor old man, perfectly exhausted! He wasn't in a state to invent a plausible story. . . . What a confidant you chose there. . . ! My husband was furious! He said: 'We can't interfere now.' So we sat down to wait. It was awful. And this poor child running over here publicly with her hair loose. She has been seen by people in the fields. She has roused the whole household, too. It's awkward for her. Luckily you are to be married next week. . . . Adèle, sit up. He has come home on his own legs, thank God. . . . We expected you to come back on a stretcher perhaps – what do I know? Go and see if the carriage is ready. I must take this child to her mother at once. It isn't proper for her to stay here a minute longer."

General D'Hubert did not move. It was as though he had heard nothing. Madame Léonie changed her mind.

"I will go and see to it myself," she said. "I want also to get my cloak . . . Adèle . . ." she began, but did not say "sit up." She went out saying in a loud, cheerful tone: "I leave the door open."

General D'Hubert made a movement towards the divan, but then Adèle sat up and that checked him dead. He thought, "I haven't washed this morning. I must look like an old tramp. There's earth on the back of my coat, and pine needles in my hair." It occurred to him that the situation required a good deal of circumspection on his part.

"I am greatly concerned, mademoiselle," he began timidly, and abandoned that line. She was sitting up on the divan with her cheeks unusually pink, and her hair brilliantly fair, falling all over her shoulders – which was a very novel sight to the general. He walked away up the room and, looking out of the window for safety, said: "I fear you must think I behaved like a madman," in accents of sincere despair. . . . Then he spun round and noticed that she had followed him with her eyes. They were not cast down on meeting his glance. And the expression of her face was novel to him also. It was, one might have said, reversed. Her eyes looked at him with grave thoughtfulness, while the exquisite lines of her mouth seemed to suggest a restrained smile. This change made her transcendental beauty much less mysterious, much more accessible to a man's comprehension. An amazing ease of mind came to the general – and even some ease of manner. He walked down the room with as much pleasurable excitement as he would have found in walking up to a battery vomiting death, fire, and smoke, then stood looking down with smiling eyes at the girl whose marriage with him (next week) had been so carefully arranged by the wise, the good, the admirable Léonie.

"Ah, mademoiselle," he said in a tone of courtly deference. "If I could be certain that you did not come here this morning only from a sense of duty to your mother!"

He waited for an answer, imperturbable but inwardly elated. It came in a demure murmur, eyelashes lowered with fascinating effect.

"You mustn't be *méchant* as well as mad."

And then General D'Hubert made an aggressive movement towards the divan which nothing could check. This piece of furniture was not exactly in the line of the open door. But Madame Léonie, coming back wrapped up in a light cloak and carrying a lace shawl on her arm for Adèle to hide her incriminating hair under, had a vague impression of her brother getting-up from his knees.

"Come along, my dear child," she cried from the doorway.

The general, now himself again in the fullest sense, showed the readiness of a resourceful cavalry officer and the peremptoriness of a leader of men.

"You don't expect her to walk to the carriage," he protested. "She isn't fit. I will carry her downstairs."

This he did slowly, followed by his awed and respectful sister. But he rushed back like a whirlwind to wash away all the signs of the night of anguish and the morning of war, and to put on the festive garments of a conqueror before hurrying over to the other house. Had it not been for that, General D'Hubert felt capable of mounting a horse and pursuing his late adversary in order simply to embrace him from excess of happiness. "I owe this piece of luck to that stupid brute," he thought. "This duel has made plain in one morning what might have taken me years to find out – for I am a timid fool. No self-confidence whatever. Perfect coward. And the Chevalier! Dear old man!" General D'Hubert longed to embrace him, too.

The Chevalier was in bed. For several days he was much indisposed. The men of the empire, and the post-revolution young ladies, were too much for him. He got up the day before the wedding, and being curious by nature, took his niece aside for a quiet talk. He advised her to find out from her husband the true story of the affair of honor, whose claim so imperative and so persistent had led her to within an ace of tragedy. "It is very proper that his wife should know. And next month or so will be your time to learn from him anything you ought to know, my dear child."

Later on when the married couple came on a visit to the mother of the bride, Madame la Générale D'Hubert made no difficulty in communicating to her beloved old uncle what she had learned without any difficulty from her husband. The Chevalier listened with profound attention to the end, then took a pinch of snuff, shook the grains of tobacco off the frilled front of his shirt, and said calmly: "And that's all what it was."

"Yes, uncle," said Madame la Générale, opening her pretty eyes very wide. "Isn't it funny? *C'est insensé* – to think what men are capable of."

"H'm," commented the old *émigré.* "It depends what sort of men. That Bonaparte's soldiers were savages. As a wife, my dear, it is proper for you to believe implicitly what your husband says."

But to Léonie's husband the Chevalier confided his true opinion. "If that's the tale the fellow made up for his wife, and during the honeymoon, too, you may depend on it no one will ever know the secret of this affair."

Considerably later still, General D'Hubert judged the time come, and the opportunity propitious to write a conciliatory letter to General Feraud. "I have never," protested the General Baron D'Hubert, "wished for your death during all the time of our deplorable quarrel. Allow me to give you back in all form your forfeited life. We two, who have been partners in so much military glory, should be friendly to each other publicly."

The same letter contained also an item of domestic information. It was alluding to this last that General Feraud answered from a little village on the banks of the Garonne:

"If one of your boy's names had been Napoleon, or Joseph, or even Joachim, I could congratulate you with a better heart. As you have thought proper to name him Charles Henri Armand I am confirmed in my conviction that you never loved the emperor. The thought of that sublime hero chained to a rock in the middle of a savage ocean makes life of so little value that I would receive with positive joy your instructions to blow my brains out. From suicide I consider myself in honor debarred. But I keep a loaded pistol in my drawer."

Madame la Générale D'Hubert lifted up her hands in horror after perusing that letter.

"You see? He won't be reconciled," said her husband. "We must take care that he never, by any chance, learns where the money he lives on comes from. It would be simply appalling."

"You are a *brave homme*, Armand," said Madame la Générale appreciatively.

"My dear, I had the right to blow his brains out – strictly speaking. But as I did not we can't let him starve. He has been deprived of his pension for 'breach of military discipline' when he broke bounds to fight his last duel with me. He's crippled with rheumatism. We are bound to take care of him to the end of his days. And, after all, I am indebted to him for the radiant discovery that you loved me a little – you sly person. Ha! Ha! Two miles, running all the way. . . ! It is extraordinary how all through this affair that man has managed to engage my deeper feelings."

The End

www.ingramcontent.com/pod-product-compliance
Lightning Source LLC
Chambersburg PA
CBHW030418310726
48979CB00007B/1107

* 9 7 8 1 6 0 6 6 4 9 6 5 7 *